Millie Barton is a Catastrophe!

Adam Strange

Copyright © 2020 by Adam Strange

First paperback edition April 2020

Book design by SMG

www.strangemediagroup.com

ISBN: 9798637495917

For Tamara, Zara, and Yasmin:
The most extraordinary adventurers
I could ever wish for x

CONTENTS

The Lion Tamer

There was never any doubt whatsoever that Millie Barton was going to be a lion tamer. At least, not in her own mind. Her parents had other ideas.

"The world will always need accountants, Millicent," said her mum.

"And supermarket retail offers great rewards, darling, how about that?" said her dad.

Millie's Mum was sub-regional manager for a high-street bank. Her Dad worked in the local supermarket, as head of frozen foods and canned vegetables. She wondered whether these facts, and her parents' opinions, may be connected. She was already feeling grumpy, as the conversation was taking place during a family dinner of over-cooked steak and kidney pie (dark brown), lumpy mashed potato (light brown), and soggy boiled cauliflower (suspiciously brown), which may explain her own particularly passionate reaction, which was to silently scream "BUT THOSE ARE THE MOST UTTERLY TEDIOUS JOBS IN THE WHOLE ENTIRE WORLD, YOU BORING BUMHEADS!" In any case, she knew she had quite a fight on her hands if she were to stand the slightest chance of deciding her own future.

"Okay, so maybe I don't have to be a lion tamer *exactly*," she reasoned, "but I want to do something exciting! And I want to be outside! And I want to spend my time with animals!"

If you knew Millie, you'd agree that these ambitions would certainly suit her personality. She was desperate to get out into the open air every day, hiding out and making dens in the bushes of the local park and trying (and failing) to get the squirrels, ducks and even pigeons to let her pet them. She was what her kinder teachers called 'a free spirit', and her parents called 'an uncontrollable feral tearaway'.

"Excitement gets you nowhere," her Mum declared. "You're going to have to start lowering your expectations at some stage, so you might as well begin now." And with that, she stood up and started clearing away the remains of their questionable meal.

Millie's older brother Josh smirked at her from across the table. He'd started this conversation by announcing his own wish to work for video game company Sun Flash when he left school. To say Josh was a gamer was an understatement of gigantic proportions. He was obsessed with gaming to such an extent that there wasn't a single room in the Barton's house that didn't have a device of some sort tucked away in it somewhere. He even had an ancient smart phone tucked behind the toilet of their downstairs loo, which Millie thought was horribly unhygienic but promised not to tell their parents about, as long as he didn't tell them about her secret collection of feathers, which he'd discovered around the same time and found equally gross. He also wore a gaming headset all the time. Like, *all* the time. Even in bed. But their parents hadn't complained about *his* choice of career, which was as unfair as it was completely bloomin' typical of them. Despite spending his entire life with a screen in front of him, the fact that Josh's ideal job involved working for the richest company in the world was enough to pull the wool over Maurice and Genevieve Barton's eyes and convince them that their son's financial future was secure. Millie narrowed her eyes at him. Although of course he didn't notice, as before he'd even put down his knife and fork his handheld Sun Flash Gamebox had appeared in his hands and he was off, weaving his way back to his

3

room without looking up once – not even when he tripped up over the edge of the kitchen rug and nearly headbutted the door frame.

After helping her Dad to clear the rest of the dinner things away, Millie headed outside to the back garden to see if she could find any feathers to add to her impressive collection, which currently numbered three hundred and sixty-one. She was hoping to get to her three hundred and sixty fifth trophy before her twelfth birthday, having started her mission as soon as she'd turned eleven. It was the sort of sunny evening that often appears just at the point where the school summer holidays are around the corner, before being replaced by mizzly and grey ones on the last day of term. The sort that teases you. Not that Millie cared, of course. Even with rain plastering her long, curly brown hair to her face, or gale-force winds whipping it into an unstraightenable mess, she'd be out and about, reaching her arms around the branches of the tallest tree she could find, or squeezing her slim frame along the bed of the brook that wound its way along the bottom of the Barton's garden. She wasn't the tallest person in her class by any, well, stretch, but she had an instinctive springiness in her bones that she used to her advantage, and managed to clamber up to lookout spots and down to hidden hollows that even the most curious cat would struggle to reach.

As she hunted for a feathery treasure (she

eventually found a beautiful bright green one that had once belonged to a Parakeet resting on the mat that surrounded her trampoline), she thought again about her future. She *had* to do something with her life that allowed her to be outdoors, to explore the world around her. To be an *adventurer*.

Little did she know that the very next day she'd take one huge step towards that dream becoming a reality.

A Shabby Shop

Millie lived in a village called Harpleford, which was about as ordinary a place as you could possibly imagine. It had a small village green with a murky fishpond in the middle of it, a village hall that was mainly used by the retired residents for table tennis clubs and Zumba classes, a playground containing two broken swings and a climbing frame, and a high street made up of mostly Italian restaurants, for some strange reason. The few other shops were remarkably unremarkable – a chemist, a post office, two nail bars, and a hairdresser – and there were a few other businesses that had closed down in recent years, leaving the premises vacant and slowly falling into disrepair.

One of these buildings had recently been opened up again, and even though the owner had somehow managed to make it look as though it was already about to close back down, Millie was fascinated by it. This was because, despite the windows being grimier than they'd been when it was a working shop before, if you squeezed yourself right up against them and squinted a bit, you could see what looked very much like animal cages on the dusty shelves.

It was the afternoon of the second Saturday of the month, which meant that Millie's Mum was getting her roots done at Frizzie's Hair Salon. Her Dad was working a shift at the supermarket, and Josh was 'researching the latest output from the gaming industry' (or playing the latest shoot-em-up on his Sun Flash Gamebox, in other words). So Millie had a precious hour to herself, which she decided would be put to good use investigating this curious new arrival in Harpleford. The shop, if you could call it that, was sandwiched between Bluebells Boutique, which sold horribly frilly dresses for over-indulged girls, and a closed-down café called Pops (the bottom of the second p had been pulled off by someone leaving it looking more like the word Poos, which might explain why customers had stopped visiting). It was so tightly squeezed in between its neighbours it was surprising it fitted at all, really – a dark green, narrow door stood to the right of a dirty window through which only the dimmest light could be seen, while the bricks were stained a very dark brown, and the roof above had long ago given up any hope of remaining pointed, turning into more of an 'n' shape than the upside down 'v' it should've been. There was no sign on the wall above the window, but instead the name of the shop was displayed on a badly cut square of wood that swung forlornly from a pole above the door. Even after crossing the road and standing almost directly below it, Millie couldn't quite be certain what the two words on it read, as the letters had been painted on in the spideriest handwriting she'd ever seen. After screwing up her eyes for a minute (drawing some fairly strange looks from passers-by), she decided that the second word probably 'Emporium'. But the first spelled something like 'Criceta', which didn't make any sense to her at all. Overall, the shop front looked as if it was actively discouraging people from going in; if it could speak, it would be saying "nothing to see here, move along now, I am incredibly dull and probably a bit stinky." But Millie had a feeling that beneath the grime, the wobbly sign, and the gloomy green door, there might be something interesting to investigate. So she pushed against the door once (it squeaked a bit, but didn't shift), then twice (it squeaked again, and wobbled this time), and three times, at which point it finally opened with a groan that told her in no uncertain terms that it didn't want to be disturbed and that she was incredibly rude for being so demanding.

Millie liked to think of herself as bold and fearless, but her bravery was tested like never before as soon as she crossed the threshold. If anything, the place was even darker on this side of the door than it had appeared when she'd been looking through the window. It felt smaller, too, with metal shelves full of animal cages lining the walls either side of her and barely enough space for two people to pass each other in the small patch of grubby lino that made up the floor in front of the service desk. Not that there'd be any danger of two customers being in the shop at one time, Millie thought, as beyond the sticky door and the dingy light there was one thing that would make any normal person think twice before remaining in the shop for more than a few seconds – the stomach-churning stench. Now, Millie was no stranger to pongs. Her brother's room ponged after a 24-hour gaming session. Her Dad's feet ponged after a particularly busy day at the supermarket. Her school canteen ponged on boiled chicken and cabbage Thursdays. But she'd have given anything to have all of these scents flooding her nose right now if it meant she didn't have to bear this. This was not a pong. This was a honking, nostril-flaring, vomit-making cocktail of nasal nastiness. Imagine, if you can, the smell of a rotten egg. Now imagine the smell of a banana that you'd left in the bottom of your schoolbag over the summer holidays, slowly getting squashed by your pencil case. Now imagine the smell of a humungous, freshly released dog poo. Now add all three smells together. This was a bit like that. It took every last bit of her willpower to keep her feet on the ground and not swivel on her heel and launch herself back onto the street, gasping for fresher air.

No bell had tinkled, or buzzer sounded, as she entered. But the creaking of the door must have alerted the shopkeeper to her entry, because just as she'd got used to the smell, a raggedy curtain behind the till separating the front from the back of the shop rustled a little, and was slowly brushed to the side by the most extraordinary looking human being Millie had ever seen.

Mr Pitts

Standing in front of Millie was a man for whom the word 'bizarre' might have been invented. He was no taller than the top of the cash register on the service desk; if he'd been standing behind it when you entered the shop, you'd have probably thought it was empty. His face wasn't exactly unfriendly, but it didn't suggest he'd be inviting you for a nice cup of tea and a slice of cake any time soon, either. Millie thought he resembled a Meerkat, with inquisitive and attentive eyes peeking out from behind a pair of thick tortoiseshell glasses, or perhaps a permanently surprised Koala. His clothes didn't smarten things up either, in fact they simply added to the overall impression created by the shop itself. His stained green hooded cardigan and frayed beige trousers were so scruffy he looked as though he'd been dragged through an entire garden centre full of bushes backwards, forwards, sideways and upside-down. And when Millie's gaze reached the top of his head, that impression was only made even stronger. His bushy ball of tightly curled jet-black hair stuck out at every angle imaginable, and appeared to have been brushed and backcombed with a handful of twigs, grass and straw. Much of this debris remained stuck to his head, and some of it, unless she was mistaken, looked very much as though it contained animal droppings. He stood there staring at her for a few uncomfortable moments, before a squeak from one of the cages jolted him into action.

"You're not supposed to be here!"

Millie was perplexed. "Er, I'm sorry, sir. I don't quite know what you mean by not being *supposed* to be here, but I'd sort of assumed I was *allowed* to be here, as there's that sign above the door, and the door was open, and, well, I don't mean to be rude but it looks as though you've got something stuck in your hair which is quite distracting…"

A few long strands of dry grass that had been poking out of the hair on the shopkeeper's forehead had begun to droop while Millie was speaking, to the point at which they were now entirely covering one of his eyes. He didn't appear to have noticed this fact.

"Hrmphh. Well, er, it must be, ah, straw from the cages," he muttered, pulling it free. "Who are you, and what are you doing here, anyway?"

Millie was taken aback by such a grumpy greeting and must have looked as surprised as she felt, as after a moment he briefly crossed his eyes before clearing his throat and starting again.

"Sorry," he said, gruffly, "I was buried in some ah, animal maintenance, and, er, must've forgotten where I am. Which is a shop. Yes, definitely a shop. A pet shop. I am in a pet shop." He seemed to be saying this to himself, almost as a reminder.

He crossed his eyes again, then "Pitts!" he shouted at her, sticking out a hand and attempting what he clearly thought was a smile but looked more to Millie like the sort of face you end up with if you hook your fingers into the sides of your mouth and pull them apart as far as you can.

"Mr Armitage Pitts of Criceta's Emporium. Pleasure to meet you! Please do feel free to tell me your name, although I can't promise I'll remember it."

Millie, whose nose had become as used to the rotten smell as it was ever going to by now, smiled to herself. *Armitage Pitts...Arm Pits*, she thought, *that's a pretty fitting name for a man who runs a shop as whiffy as this one*. She couldn't help but be intrigued by this Mr Pitts, though, and her inquisitive nature made her determined to find out as much as she could about

13

him. It felt as though he was acting the role of a shopkeeper, remembering the lines and actions he was supposed to take instead of actually wanting to do it. She decided to test him a bit more.

"It's a pleasure to meet you too, Mr Pitts, and welcome to Harpleford. My name's Millie – well, Millicent really but nobody ever calls me that – and I'd like to begin our acquaintance by asking you a few questions if I may: Do you mind me asking what made you choose my village as the home for your business venture? Why does your shop have such an unusual name? And what pets do you sell here? I can only see rodent cages and to be honest, I like cats the most, but my parents won't let me have one so I might be willing to settle for something else if you can convince me."

Mr Pitts furrowed his brows tightly for a long time, as though he were trying to come up with a normal answer. Then he stared at her for an even longer time, with an intensity that she'd never seen before. Not even during the staring contest that took place when she'd briefly dangled Josh's favourite games console out of her bedroom window during a particularly stormy argument. He opened his mouth. A few seconds passed. He coughed. A few more seconds passed. He crossed his eyes again. Then:

"Cats, eh? Yes, I suppose there's something feline in your features. Interesting... Oh fudge it! It's no use, young lady. I can see from the sparks behind those bright green eyes of yours that you're not going to let me bluff my way out of this. I came here because of the soil. I sell hamsters. And the shop is called Criceta's because of them; it means 'hamster' in latin, you see. You've obviously worked out that this is a somewhat unusual pet shop. But before I can tell you anything more about it, I'll have to know if I can trust you. Now, please watch my left hand very carefully…"

With this, Mr Pitts thrust his *right* hand, in which he was holding a stubby pencil, upwards and out to the side. Millie ignored it.

"You're paying attention! Good." He scribbled something down on a notepad that lay on the countertop beside him.

Next, he waved his left hand up and down, around in circles one way then the other, then backwards and forwards across Millie's field of vision until she was dizzy with exertion and her eyes ached. Finally, he stopped, and reached out again to write something in his pad.

"I'm delighted to say that you can indeed be trusted!" he exclaimed with a smile. "You told me with your own eyes, you see – watch this." Millie watched as Mr Pitts edged past her and started waving his hand around in exactly the same motion as he'd been using before, but this time using the stubby end of his pencil to mark out the lines, loops and swirls in the grime on the back of the front door of the shop. When he'd finished, he stepped back with a proud "Ta-da!"

Millie realised that all that waving and waggling hadn't been as random as it had appeared. Now she could see it in physical form on the door it became clear that Mr Pitts had been writing the phrase 'I promise that I am entirely trustworthy and shall keep the secrets that Mr Armitage Pitts is about to tell me' in the air.

"So, you see, you've made me what we call an 'eyeball agreement' here, and those must never be broken!" he said. "But just to be sure, I'd appreciate it if you could do things the old-fashioned way here, as well." He'd scribbled the same phrase down on the pad on the counter as a record, and got her to sign it.

At that exact moment a clock chimed from somewhere behind the curtain. Mr Pitts' eyebrows shot up until they were practically buried underneath his bush of hair.

"Come back next Saturday if you want to know more about all of this! 13:45 on the dot! And bring a toothbrush!"

Sun Flash

Hamsters? Bring a toothbrush?

Millie's mind boggled as she attempted to make sense out of the strange little man's words. She walked in a daze to Frizzie's Hair Salon where she was due to meet her mum. She tried very hard to process everything she'd seen, heard and of course smelled, but before she'd had a chance to fully digest her experience, her thoughts were interrupted by Genevieve Barton bursting out of the salon, her hair so voluminous it would put a pedigree poodle to shame.

"Do you like it?" she asked. "I thought it might be a little *alternative* for the bank, but Dorian persuaded me. He pointed out that I *am* sub-regional manager now, after all – told me I've got to make a statement.

Ha! Like a bank statement, you see? He's *such* a wag!"
Dorian, her long-standing hairdresser and confidante,
always managed to get Mum into a good mood, and
rather than risk spoiling that Millie decided to keep
quiet about what she'd been up to, instead letting
herself get swept along with Mum's plans for the rest
of the day, which included such exciting treats as
hunting for yellow label price-reduced bargains at the
supermarket, coffee and cake with her reading group
friends, and a trip to the local DIY store. Sunday
passed in its usual, predictable pattern of homework,
housework and a dreaded Sunday roast (or Sunday
Groast, as she preferred to call it), so it wasn't long
until Mr Pitts and his peculiar Emporium really were
put to the back of Millie's mind.

Millie's school was a very short walk from the
house - her parents were obsessed with something
called 'catchment areas', and were delighted when a
few years ago they'd managed to buy a home so close
to school it apparently meant other people would pay
way more than it was worth if and when they
eventually sold it. (Millie couldn't help wondering
whether her parents had therefore paid way more
than it was worth when *they* bought it but didn't dare
ask as she knew she'd get a long and rambling answer,
and frankly life was too short for that sort of subject.)
Harpleford High managed to squeeze in nearly two
thousand pupils, and it was a constant source of

disappointment to Millie that almost all of them seemed perfectly happy to look the same, act the same, and share the same opinions as each other. They all attempted the same acts of rebellion against the school uniform, making their ties as stubby as possible, hoiking their skirts up above the knee, and popping their blazer collars (although thankfully a ridiculous phase that had involved the boys keeping one trouser leg rolled up to reveal the most garish sock they could get away with was short-lived). They also all listened to the same music, followed the same sports, and obsessed over the same celebrities, TV shows, youtubers, and gadgets.

That Monday, Millie and Josh headed into school to be greeted by the sight of two enormous inflatable sun-shaped balloons with sunglasses perched on top, looming high over the entrance gates. Not only that, there was also a sleek, silver helicopter parked in the middle of the school tennis courts in the distance. Josh nearly wet himself. In fact, from the slightly confused look that briefly passed across his face Millie was almost certain her brother must have had a small 'accident'.

"SUN FLASH! IT'S SUN FLASH!" he yelled as he attempted to sprint to the main school doors. Unsurprisingly for someone who was glued to a screen for every available minute of the day, Josh didn't have a great deal of strength in any part of his body other than his thumbs, which were crushingly strong (as Millie had discovered during a thumb war challenge) from all the tapping, tweaking, pushing and pulling they were put through on his consoles. So for him, running consisted of taking about a dozen steps before stitch set in, his puny chest started heaving like a little sparrow's, and his brittle legs started to wobble. He sat down on a wall beside the gate clutching his sides, while Millie caught up. As in so many other ways, the siblings were completely different animals in this respect; neither was particularly large (probably due to horrible food they had to suffer at home), but with Millie spending so much time outside, clambering up trees and crawling around in the undergrowth, she could run, hike, cycle or swim for hours, and her slight frame hid a strength that would put a gorilla to shame.

"Careful, Josh," Millie warned, "I've got a feeling you're going to need every last over-excited breath in your body to get through whatever this lot have got to say for themselves today."

"Shut up, Mill-Billy, you're just jealous because I'm going to be a multi-billionaire by the time I'm twenty thanks to these guys," Josh retorted. Mill-Billy was his *hilarious* insult for Millie, based on the fact she was more interested in being outside, which in his view made her as stupid as the redneck cowboys with the funny accents he'd seen on old American cartoons, called Hillbillies. It wasn't hilarious. It was completely pathetic, and it was as ignorant a view of them as it was of her, but Millie had learned that pointing such things out only made him taunt her more.

The reason for Josh's behaviour was that it looked like for once a school rumour was actually coming true. As everyone knows, rumours in a school are like nits in a, well, school. They spread like crazy and only stop when a responsible adult steps in and pours cold water (or medicated shampoo) on them. The story that Sun Flash were going to come and give one of their famous 'Fun and Freebie' roadshows at Harpleford was probably about the 3,714th supposedly secret thing that was going to happen this term, so nobody had really believed it until now. Yet here they were, and predictably, Josh wasn't the only excitable pupil in the vicinity. Millie found herself in the middle of a human wave of bodies flooding excitedly towards the school, when normally on a Monday fellow students would be stopping in the playground to rearrange their bags, adjust the zips on their coats, re-tie their shoelaces, or do anything they could think of to delay the moment at which they had to cross the threshold.

Sun Flash Games called itself the 'Funderbolt of the digital age'. Once the biggest gaming company in the world, it was now the biggest company in the world, full stop, and as a result it managed to buy its way into schools, libraries, and even hospitals, supposedly supporting the community but – to Millie's mind at least – conveniently managing to sell even more of their products along the way.

This morning, the entire school population was ushered into the hall for assembly after registration, to find the huge space covered in Sun Flash posters, flags and bunting, with a stack of enormous speakers and a huge screen set up on the stage. After a horribly gushing introduction, thanking the company for its generous donation of (heavily branded) tablets for every classroom, the headteacher, Mrs Bland, informed the students that Harpleford High was exceptionally fortunate to have been granted an educational talk by one of the world's most successful entrepreneurs, and instructed them to show their appreciation in the usual way. With this, she hurried from the stage, and, to a chorus of cheering and stamping from 2,000 pairs of pupil-sized hands and feet, on walked the man who'd brought this whole show to Harpleford.

"Welllllllcome Steeeeyewdennnnnnnts! Arrrrre yeeeeewwww ready for a FUNDERBOLT?"

The voice that bellowed these barely intelligible words didn't really need to be amplified by a microphone. It was already boomier and screechier than the angriest parent you can possibly imagine, telling off the naughtiest child you can possibly imagine, after discovering they'd committed the most awful crime you can possibly imagine. But it was being broadcast into a headset that was clamped around an oddly small mouth that sat beneath a curiously round nose, intense blue eyes and a startlingly blond quiff, on the perfectly circular, perfectly pink face of one perfectly obese man called Jeremiah Trooper. Trooper was the CEO and owner of Sun Flash, having started the company from his bedroom in the small apartment in New York in which he'd been brought up. According to the numerous articles that had been written about Trooper, his parents had been successful lawyers in the city and were rarely home when he was a child, so he'd focused all his energy on creating make-believe worlds on the various computers and devices they'd thrown his way to keep him busy and, probably, make themselves feel less guilty about spending so little time with him.

Whatever the reality was behind this story, though, you couldn't doubt his enthusiasm for the company he founded; even beyond the bright pink sheen of his face he radiated excitement about the products that had made him his fortune.

"Kiddos! Pin those ears back and listen to me!" Trooper commanded, somewhat unnecessarily given that his thick American accent was being broadcast into every nook and cranny of the room. "There is nothing in this world as important as video game technology. Nothing! And heck, shouldn't I know it! Gaming transformed my life, and it's going to transform yours. It's more important than your friends, your family, and anything you learn here, or in the so-called 'outside world'. It's the world *inside our devices* that counts, and I'm going to prove to you just how life-changing it can be."

Millie scanned the audience around her. A few of the teachers were sharing uneasy glances, but everyone else was transfixed.

"At midnight your British time, on the very last day of this month, across the entire world, we are launching our revolutionary Flash Pack!" At this point the audience gasped, as a 3D image of a brown paper parcel with a question mark hovering above it began rotating on the screen at the back of the stage. Trooper smiled to himself.

"The Flash Pack will be able to play all of your favourite Sun Flash games of course, Redneck's Revenge, Who Wants to be a Billionaire, Race to the Bottom, and all those other great pieces of art we've brought your way over the years. And every device will also come pre-loaded with a very special new release: TROOPER'S TREASURE TUNNEL, a shoot 'em up, shoot 'em down never-ending adventure quest set across an infinite number of worlds and set in the future, the past, and the present day featuring a cast of millions of characters." The audience gasped some more as Trooper drew breath.

"You know what, though? That's not even the best bit." His voice dropped to a whisper, which was such a shock to the system after the volume of the rest of his speech that one of the Year 7s in the audience actually let out a small squeak of relief. "As you'd expect from a visionary like me, the Flash Pack will contain the very latest 5G, mixed reality technology, so the so-called 'real world' won't have to get in the way of your game time so much. But even more amazingly, this revolutionary, radical reinvention of the hand-held gaming device world will never need charging, will never need to have its batteries replaced, because it will be…" he paused, "unturnoffable.

"Yes, I know that's not a word, and I also know that having a device around the house or school that doesn't ever shut down might upset a few of the *older* folks" – here he nodded his head in the direction of the teachers, winning a small chorus of laughs from a handful of cocky Year 10s – "but it *has* to be unturnoffable. Always on. Always playable. Because after the game has been running for exactly one year, whichever brave, patient, committed, player has clocked up more hours and gained more points than ANYONE ELSE ON THE PLANET, will be the very first recipient of 'Trooper's Trillion'! And if you're wondering what that is, let me show you…"

Trooper's Trillion

At this point the rotating 3D parcel image burst open and started flooding the screen with a never-ending stream of virtual dollar bills. Trooper's speech continued.

"Yes, that's right, I am giving the winner of the game ONE TRILLION dollars as a prize. That's nearly eight hundred billion pounds to you British folks! On a summer's day like today you could buy four hundred billion ice creams with it! Heck, you could buy 10 million ice cream vans if you wanted to…"

The hall was in uproar. Trooper stood on the stage, smiling widely at the fever he'd created, before patting down the air in front of his outstretched arms until the noise eventually calmed down.

"I'm glad you think it's as special as I do, folks," he said, before a strange, serious, and to Millie's eyes at least, sinister look appeared in his beady eyes.

"That's all I've got time for; now the word's out I've gotta get back in my chopper out there and tour the world telling other folks about the deal. But before I go, let me leave you with a little advice. Get as much sleep as you can between now and the end of the month. Rush your homework. Gobble your food. Stock up on sweets, chocolate bars and sugary drinks, because you ain't gonna want to sleep when the Flash Pack hits these shores. 'If you're sleeping, you'll end up weeping', as I like to say, as I can guarantee there'll be someone out there who's propping their eyelids open and racing ahead of you to get that prize."

Then, with the smile turned back on and a cacophony of streamer rockets and fanfare music filling the hall, he turned on his heels and trotted off the stage, out of sight. Almost immediately, the deep bass sound of the helicopter's engine gearing up filtered into the room, reaching a crescendo before gradually quietening as the craft and its trillionaire occupant flew into the distance. The hall was silent again, the crowd inside completely shell-shocked.

The teachers started gathering their classes and ushering them out; almost all of them looked very queasy, as this was very much not what they'd been expecting, but what could they do? Trooper had delivered the message he'd wanted to bring, the children were hooked on the idea, and the last two weeks of the school year were destined to be void of any learning whatsoever. Millie glanced across at Josh, whose face was fixed in a rapturous daze, contemplating the glorious future that lay before him. She felt the opposite. Although she couldn't quite put her finger on the reason for it, she had a worrying feeling that Jeremiah Trooper wasn't quite as generous as he was claiming to be.

Nan Barton

The rest of the school week passed in a blur of over-excited distraction and very little learning. Millie's teachers failed miserably to get the class to focus on anything, such was the pupils' feverish excitement about the Sun Flash announcement. It wasn't exactly helped by the fact that the company's publicity machine had now kicked into gear as well, flooding social media, the internet and television with news and speculation about the new Flash Pack console and the technology that made it work without ever needing to be charged. The only lesson in which some semblance of order was maintained was ICT, and that was because the pupils managed to surreptitiously browse the web for further gossip about the game on the school computers. Millie was relieved when Saturday came around, although she had her fortnightly visit to Nan's house to get through before she could make her return to the intriguing pet shop.

Nan Barton was Millie's grandmother on her Dad's side, and she'd lived alone since Millie's Grandad had died five years earlier. She was 86 years old, seemed to be getting an inch shorter for every inch Millie grew taller, and reminded Millie of a sparrow, with shrewd, inquisitive eyes and a sharp mind that didn't miss a thing. Millie loved her dearly, and enjoyed their conversations. But she couldn't help but be frustrated by the fact that her visits (which were rotated with Josh, who went on the weekends she didn't go) meant spending half a day indoors, as Nan had undergone a major operation two years ago and hadn't been able to walk without using a frame since. At least her cooking was better than her parents'; she'd roamed the world in her younger years and after her operation she'd stated that she was going to go 'travelling by tastebud' instead, cooking experimental food from across the globe.

This weekend's taste experience was from Africa – a dish called Bunny Chow that consisted of an exceptionally hot curry housed in half a hollowed-out loaf of bread. While Millie was cautiously prodding at it with her fork, she regaled her Nan with news of the week's events.

"It's all just so frustrating, Nan; hardly anyone's interested in playing outside with me as it is and now this stupid game's coming along it's going to be impossible to drag them away from their new consoles. I'm beginning to think I'm more of a weirdo than Josh. Maybe he's the normal child and I'm the one who doesn't fit." She put down her fork and gulped, holding back the tears that were threatening to spill.

"Now listen here, Millicent," said Nan, using Millie's full name as she only did when she was about to say something Really Serious. "There's absolutely nothing wrong with being different. Just think, if there weren't fantastic people like you in the world to appreciate and enjoy the wonderful sights, sounds and smells that the earth itself has to offer us without any interference from the human race, the planet would be in even more trouble than it is already. Your grandad always used to say that, and for once I couldn't agree with him more. Life might feel a bit lonely at the moment, but wait and see – you're going to do some remarkable things in your time, and the world will thank you for it. You mark my words, young lady."

Millie thought about this for a moment. Nan's words were certainly encouraging, but how could she be so sure that an exciting life awaited when the rest of her granddaughter's life could hardly be any more *un*remarkable?

"Nan?"

"Yes, darling?"

"Has Dad always been so, well, so *ordinary*? It's just that you understand how I feel better than anyone else, and you sound like you're pretty sure that my life is going to go in a different direction to his and mum's, and although he hardly ever shows it I sometimes see him looking a bit, like, dreamy, and because he's your son and you're so much more exciting than him I just sort of wondered…"

"If he's hiding something?" Nan interrupted. She paused before continuing.

"Well, he's always asked me not to talk about this but now we're on the subject I can't help thinking it's time for me to tell you, as long as you promise you'll keep it a secret."

"Keep what a secret, Nan?"

"You're quite correct, as it happens, Millie. Your Dad didn't want to be a supermarket shelf stacker when he was a young man. In fact, he was almost as adventurous as you when he was your age. In those days we didn't worry quite so much about where our youngsters were outside of school, and what they got up to, but I couldn't begin to tell you the number of times I shouted myself hoarse trying to get him to come back in from the fields beyond our back garden to eat his dinner. Anyway, there was one event in his teenage years that changed his life forever – for better at first, then for worse.

"A circus came to visit the area one year, and set up camp on the common for a whole week. Dad had a bit of pocket money saved up, and went to watch it on the first night. He came back a different person! He loved it so much he bought a ticket for the next day on his way out, and did that for the whole week. Grandad wasn't happy about him spending all his savings so frivolously, but I persuaded him that if Dad came to regret it, he'd at least have learnt a useful lesson.

"There was one act that Dad was particularly in awe of - the sword swallower. Apparently, the performer who did it got some of the biggest cheers of the night, and I think there was something about the way in which they'd managed to make their outwardly ordinary body do something so inwardly spectacular that really appealed to him. He decided to learn how to do it himself, secretly taking himself off to the library to read about the theory behind the art, then heading down to the woods on the edge of town to practise his technique with the straightest sticks he could find. He only told us about it a couple of years later, when he could do it properly, and when he was big enough and ugly enough for us not to really be able to do anything about it. And just to prove he didn't completely have his head in the clouds he informed us he was going to take his new-found talent to the town square and perform there for some extra money."

Nan paused, and her face clouded slightly. She took a deep breath and continued.

"Things went well for him at first. He'd head up to town bright and early – the best way to catch the families with young kids, he said – swallow his swords for a few hours, then pack up by the middle of the afternoon and come home in order to take off on his bike for a ride in the countryside.

"Then came the day that changed everything.

"The town was fairly quiet that weekend; it was the August bank holiday, so lots of people had headed off to the coast to catch the last of the summer's warmth. But around lunchtime, a group of girls stopped by to watch his performance. There were four of them, all about the same age as him. As you might imagine, sword swallowing is not something you can do without focusing on the job in hand, so Dad tried not to pay too much attention to them, but he'd been performing for a few hours by then and must have been a bit tired, and there was one girl, in a bright yellow dress, who he couldn't help noticing out of the corner of his eye. The other three girls started walking off, but this one loitered for a few seconds more, before being dragged away by one of her giggling friends.

"He'd never say this out loud, but I think he must have been distracted by the movement, or the giggles of the girls, as at that moment he turned his head slightly, accidentally twisting the sharp steel rod that was at that precise moment approaching the rear of his throat, and catching it on his tongue, slicing into it. He yanked the sword from his mouth and cried out, dropping to his knees in pain. The girl and her friends rushed to help him – even trying to bind up his tongue with a handkerchief – but by the time they'd got him to hospital the damage was done. The doctors told us he was extremely lucky not to have killed himself and had got away very lightly, all things considered; he'd have difficulty eating for a few months, but there'd also be some longer lasting damage to contend with, as he'd scraped off the taste buds from his tongue and there was nothing anyone could do to reattach them."

Nan stopped to dab at her eyes, which were now misting up. Millie's were, too, and her mind was racing as she started to connect the various pieces of this story with a bigger picture that was forming in her mind. It explained a couple of things quite clearly to her. First, why her Dad didn't really look as though he had his heart in it when he was telling her off for messing around outside, and why he sometimes got a melancholy look in his eyes after doing so. It also explained why he showed so little interest in cookery, and why his food was always so tasteless, although Millie realised that this wasn't the most important thing to be worrying about right now.

There was one other suspicion forming in her mind, too. One that, if it were true, would explain why *both* Millie's parents were so reluctant for her to pursue a thrill-seeking life.

"Nan?" she asked.

"Yes, darling?"

"The girl in the yellow dress. Was she my Mum?"

"Yes, darling. She was. And she's never forgiven herself."

Another Revelation

Millie's mind was reeling as she left her Nan's to catch the bus back home. She couldn't decide which emotion to focus on – sadness at her poor Dad's tragic accident and her poor Mum who must, underneath all her hard-nosed behaviour, feel wretched to this day for causing it, or relief at the fact that she no longer needed to feel quite so peculiarly different, that there *was* a reason behind her instinct for adventure and excitement. She was so distracted that she nearly missed her stop, and had to admit she was glad that she had her new acquaintance Mr Pitts' strange invitation to concentrate on, rather than hovering around at home waiting for her parents to appear and pretending everything was completely normal in front of them. They'd gone shopping in the local town and for once, Josh had gone with them.

As you might imagine, Josh would usually spend his weekends glued to the Gamebox in his room, but since the Sun Flash announcement he'd been devoting an unusually large chunk of his time preparing for the contest to start, emptying out his bank account in order to order his Flash Pack, performing weird eye-stretching and hand-clenching exercises to get himself 'match-fit', and writing lists of supplies on sticky notes. He'd jumped at the chance to join his parents in town and start stocking up at their expense. Millie hadn't paid much attention to his lists but had spotted the words 'energy drinks' written in marker pen on one scrap of paper that he'd stuck to the fridge door, with 'buy coffee machine?' scribbled below it in a slightly more hesitant hand (Mr and Mrs Barton might have been a bit overindulgent with Josh, but even they had their limits). He'd also pinned a summer holiday timetable on to his wall, in which he'd allowed himself two chunks of three hours for sleeping, with the remaining 18 hours to be spent in front of *Trooper's Treasure Tunnel*. He'd added arrows at certain points with instructions such as 'shout for mum to make me a sandwich here' and 'phone for pizza delivery using dad's voice here'. Millie spotted this on one of the rare occasions on which she'd been allowed into his room (not that she particularly ever wanted to go into that stink pit), and when she pointed out the fact that he hadn't included any slots for showering or toilet breaks he just tapped the side of his nose, mysteriously. He pointed towards a rusty old watering can and a towel that had been placed on a sheet of tarpaulin in the corner of the room. Then he pointed towards a couple of plastic buckets on the floor by the side of his bed with three jumbo-sized multi-packs of toilet roll stacked next to them. Then he pointed to an arrow that appeared on the timetable at about 9am every day with a note attached to it saying, simply, 'empty bucket, fill watering can'. She thought it best not to ask further questions after that.

As she had the house to herself, Millie was able to retrieve her toothbrush from the bathroom without anyone questioning her. This didn't stop her questioning her own sanity, though; what on earth did Mr Pitts want such a strange, small, and in Millie's case, spindly and squashed up item for, anyway? She didn't have time to worry about it though, so she popped it into her back pocket and headed back out, over to the high street and into Criceta's Emporium.

***

"Aha! I remembered! You're here! And I'm here! Well *done*, Pitts!"

These were the thoroughly over-excited and exceptionally loud words that assaulted Millie's ears as she forced her way back into the shop, having remembered to give the door an almighty shove this time. The hatch on the cash register counter was open and Mr Pitts was standing on the tiny shop floor inspecting something in one of the cages that lined the shelves as she entered, which resulted in the two of them standing nose to nose as he greeted her. Not only did this make his exclamation even more ear-burstingly loud, but it also gave Millie's nostrils a punch of pungence from his particularly unusual brand of body odour – she wasn't sure whether it was his smell that made the shop smell, or if the smell of the shop itself was rubbing off, literally, on him. If she hadn't been heading into the place at such speed, the force of the whiff alone might have pushed her backwards onto her bottom. In any case, he was clearly delighted to see her, and clearly delighted with himself for remembering his own side of the arrangement.

"Welcome back, welcome back and well done, well done for being on time, Minnie", Mr Pitts blurted next. "In this business, timing is everything!"

Millie hadn't got a clue what he was talking about. And she was a bit annoyed that he'd forgotten her name already. But she nodded anyway.

"Good. So, to address your previous questions about the reason for my appearance in Harpleford, I'm here because of the hamsters."

Mr Pitts was warming to his theme now, and getting

so overexcited that his next words came out in a tumble of noise spoken so quickly it looked like his lips were vibrating instead of forming recognisable sounds.

"More accurately, I'm here in this location because the soil is quite perfect for the precise combination of rotovation of squeezed earth filtration and cavity optimisation required in order to achieve demi-hemispherical internatural reappearance. The ground beneath our feet changes from one step to the next, you see – sometimes a minuscule amount, sometimes more than you'd think – so it's very hard to find a spot where the rocks, minerals, and soil are made up of exactly the right bits and pieces for people like me to do our jobs. With me so far?"

"Well, I'm not entirely…" Millie ventured, although Mr Pitts obviously hadn't heard as he continued.

"And the reason I *know* the soil is perfect for demi-hemispherical internatural reappearance *is*…?"

Millie kept quiet, hoping that this was not a question she was actually meant to answer.

"The hamsters, of course!" he beamed, as if telling the punchline to a joke they both knew was coming.

"Because everyone who's anyone in this business knows just how sensitive our rodent friends here are when it comes to sub-soil transference pathways. It's like carrying around a living, breathing, Sat Nav. Only instead of roads above ground, they discover routes beneath it."

Millie couldn't contain her confusion any further, although she was starting to think she might understand what he was driving at.

"Hang on, Mr Pitts," she said, loudly, in order to get his attention back. "Stop me if I'm wrong, but are you telling me that you're here because Harpleford is some sort of hot spot habitat for hamsters and that you can tell from their behaviour that they like it here? And just to remind you, my name's Mrrphsh…"

Mr Pitts had held up his hand to stop her, and given how close they were standing to each other he'd ended up completely covering her mouth with his stinky palm.

"Sorry Mickey, I appreciate I get a little over-excited on the subject of sub-soil transference. I tend to forget how few people know as much about this as I do.

"You're nearly right, but you're not remotely correct. I am here because the hamsters showed me I should be here, as they always do, by, er, farting in unison when we drove into the village. And what they and their bottom burps show me is not just that they like it here (although they do). It's that Harpleford is one of just a few places on the world's surface where the chemical and mineral make-up of the ground beneath us makes it possible to access the Underwhere, which in turn allows us *travel through the interior of the earth at remarkable speed and without any* – at least as far as we know – *long term damage to the human body!*"

"Whablublapper huh?" was all Millie could

manage to say in response to this.

"Let me put it another way. You know those maps that you get in airports and inflight magazines with lines marked on them showing you all the routes around the globe that a particular airline flies to? Well, there are routes like that beneath the surface of the earth that humans, if they're careful, can travel along in order to get to far away places quickly. Which we often do, because of the various emergencies we have to deal with.

"And before you ask – by we, I mean the Society of Extraordinary Adventurers. We're a secret organisation with members stretched across every corner of the globe. We're all a bit, er, unusual, we all have particular areas of interest, but we all have one thing in common. Every member, of every age, and every nationality, has dedicated their lives to going to extraordinary lengths to stop the selfish behaviour of the human race from destroying the planet for our fellow animals. It's an instinct, really, an urge that can't be ignored, and although the odds are stacked against us, we're never going to give up until every last animal is safe from harm."

Millie was fascinated; the feeling he was speaking about felt immediately familiar to her, and she wanted to find out more. Before she had a chance to ask him, though, he looked at his watch, and jumped.

"It's nearly time to go! Get your toothbrush out, and follow me!"

The Rotatormate
3000

Millie still had a thousand questions to ask Mr Pitts, but she thought she'd got the overall picture: essentially, he was some sort of globetrotting adventurer who used secret pathways beneath the surface of the earth to whizz from one country to another, or perhaps even one continent to another, in order to do something that sounded suspiciously like it might involve saving the earth. Or saving the human race. Or something like that. This was clearly bonkers. *He* was clearly bonkers. But, she thought, he was also quite charming in a quirky sort of way, and a bit of an oddball. And as a bit of an oddball herself, she couldn't help warming to him.

"Come on, Mildred!"

Mr Pitts had dashed through the open hatch on the counter and into the back of the shop, leaving the threadbare curtain separating the two areas rustling in his wake. Ignoring his continued inability to remember her name, Millie took as deep a breath as she could manage given the now familiar if not any less disgusting stink, and stepped forward.

The sight that greeted her as she pushed her way through the curtain was stranger than anything she'd ever dreamed. And Millie had once dreamed that she'd been carried in the pouch of an enormous kangaroo canoeing down rapids filled with melted cheese while being pursued by a herd of tiny elephants on jet skis – you can't get much weirder than that. In many ways it was just an ordinary stock room. It was about the size of the Barton's spare bedroom – longer than it was wide, windowless, and illuminated by the glare of a strip bulb stretching along the ceiling. There were boxes and crates stacked on shelves, sacks of food pellets and bedding for the hamsters piled along one wall, and a rusting, grey, dented filing cabinet slumped against another, with an old-fashioned clock hanging precariously from the wall above it. But what made it different, however; what made it so completely unlike any room Millie had ever been in before, was the object that filled most of the remaining floorspace and stretched almost all the way to the ceiling.

It was a hamster wheel. A human-sized, wooden hamster wheel with rickety slats running all the way around it and enclosed by spokes on both sides, set within a metal frame that had been screwed to the floor. This frame had two metal boxes attached to it – one where the centre of the wheel was attached to the frame, and one about halfway down one of the metal struts. Trailing out of this second box was a thick cable, snaking into a human-sized, circular hole in the floorboards, through which Millie could see nothing but an ominous blackness.

Mr Pitts waved at the strange device. "Allow me to introduce you to…" (Here he coughed, and cleared his throat), "THE ROTATORMATE 3000! Isn't she fantastic, Milky!"

Millie wasn't quite prepared to humour him by dropping to the floor in amazement at this creaky contraption, but she nonetheless managed to squeeze out a "wow" and widen her eyes to demonstrate a bit of enthusiasm. And to be fair, it *was* a pretty impressive feat of engineering, squeezing such a big structure into a poky room like this.

"She rattles a bit and some of the slats are getting a little, er, hazardous, but she does what she needs to do, and obviously she's a massive improvement on the 2000 model. Fewer, er, splattings. Ready to give her a whirl?"

"Give *what* a whirl, exactly Mr Pitts?"

"Your first International Transfer of course!" He thought to himself for a moment. "I think it's going to be best if I go first; I can set a repeater on the programming nodule and then all you'll have to do is hop on after me, get her up to speed, and she'll fire you off to join me."

He hopped over to the frame and lifted the lid of the lower box, revealing a forest of wires and switches protruding from a rubbery sphere about the size of a football. He examined the ball carefully until he found a particular switch, flicked it backwards and forwards twice, and looked at his watch.

"Excellent. It's now 13:58, so we should be at transfer velocity by 14:00. As long as you don't let her slow down too much before you jump on you should be able to transfer before the end of the four-minute window."

It evidently dawned on Mr Pitts, for once, that Millie wouldn't have a clue what he was talking about, so he explained further. "Internatural transfers aren't entirely, well, natural, so we have to limit their occurrence; every time we poke around under the surface of the earth like this we give the planet a little wobble you see, and if we do it too much it might get a little, er, angry, and show its displeasure with a few random volcanoes, earthquakes, and that sort of thing. So, we can only do the outbound journey at certain times of the day – at 09:00, 14:00, and 16:00, with an emergency option at 20:00. And we can only use the routes during a four-minute period each time.

"This..." he paused, turned, and was suddenly right in front of Millie's face "...is very important. We have rules, and if we break them our membership is revoked. Do not let that happen to *me* by missing the boat when I'm responsible for *you*. If you see that clock ticking towards 14:04 before you've got the Rotatormate 3000 up to speed I want you to jump off it. Immediately. Is that clear?"

"Crystal?" Millie offered, a little hesitantly.

"Oh, and you should probably also be aware that if you don't jump at precisely the right moment, you'll end up getting your feet stuck in the gaps between the slats and you'll be flattened like a pancake on the inside of the wheel. All the blood in your body will rush to your head, which will turn as blue as a blueberry, and you'll never be able to walk properly again because you'll be so top-heavy. But I've hardly ever seen that happen so don't worry too much about it."

"Er, Mr Pitts?"

"Yes? I hope this is a simple question Michaela, – time is travel, as they say."

She was pretty sure they didn't say this, but Millie ploughed on anyway.

"I think I understand what I'm meant to do – get on the wheel after you've finished doing whatever you're about to do on it – but why exactly do I need my toothbrush?"

"Oh yes! How silly of me to forget. Your toothbrush may be necessary for the purposes of distraction. It's an extremely unusual looking item to anyone or anything who's not seen one before, so if you find yourself sharing your landing zone with anything out of the ordinary, you can just whip it out of your pocket and brandish it in their general direction, like this…"

At this point Mr Pitts leapt backwards into an 'on guard' stance, simultaneously plucking a grimy toothbrush with extremely squashed bristles from the back pocket of his trousers and waving it so close to Millie's nose she turned cross-eyed.

"See? You know what it is already and even you were distracted! I could've run a mile while you were getting your head around what just happened."

This was certainly true.

Mr Pitts stuffed the brush back into his pocket and squeezed himself between two of the wheel's spokes so he was standing on the slats, facing the wall with the clock dangling from it. At that exact moment, the clock started to chime.

"Here we go then!" he shouted. "Time for drop-down! Good luck in the Underwhere!"

Drop-Down

Millie's whole body started to vibrate as the tremendous clattering she'd heard the first time she'd met Mr Pitts started up again. The groan was coming from the hole on the floor beneath them, as though the earth itself was having a good old moan about being so rudely interrupted from its smooth daily routine. Meanwhile, the shopkeeper was staring straight ahead, keeping the top half of his body completely still while his legs were walking, then jogging, then running on the spot while the huge wheel picked up speed beneath his feet. Despite being screwed to the floor, the frame started wobbling alarmingly once he'd built up a bit of speed, and a few prongs of wood splintered off the slats, which was even more worrying, not to mention hazardous. But once Millie had got used to the teeth-chattering sensation of the whole experience, she noticed the strangest thing. The outside of the wheel was *glowing*, faintly at first, but then brightening until it started to resemble the bright reflector panels Millie remembered her dad attaching to the spokes of her first bicycle. Before long, the low-pitched groaning coming from the ground was accompanied by much higher *wheeing* and *whooshing* noises being generated by the wheel's motion. This new sound got louder, and louder, and louder as the wheel span faster, and faster, and faster, until a light on the top metal box suddenly started flashing and a siren started wailing, at which point Mr Pitts jumped straight up in the air, clamped his hand over his nose, and dropped straight down into…

Nothing.

He jumped into nothingness.

He hadn't hit the slats and smeared himself all over them as Millie had assumed was going to happen. He hadn't broken through the outside of the wheel and plunged into the hole beneath. He hadn't even managed to throw himself out of the side of the contraption, which had been her most optimistic hope. Nope. He'd simply vanished into the stuffy, smelly air of the stock room. She edged her way around the wheel as it continued to turn, inspecting it for clues about what had happened. But even with her investigative mind in its sharpest focus, she couldn't find an answer. She stood, dumbfounded, for a moment. Then the siren stopped, and the light turned off, and she was snapped back to attention. She glanced at the clock, which was now reading two minutes past two and thirty seconds, took another big breath, and launched herself into the wheel.

It was a small miracle Millie didn't fall flat onto her backside as soon as she landed. She'd tried to imagine she was jumping on to a moving roundabout at the park, only sideways, and luckily the technique just about worked. The wheel was continuing to spin at a jogging pace, and with a few big steps she was huffing and puffing her way to a pretty impressive speed. Mr Pitts' warning words about the time were ringing in her head and she dared to glance up at the clock – three minutes past two and ten seconds... twenty... twenty-five... She started panicking. Where were the glowing spokes? Why hadn't the light come on? Where was the siren? She had less than half a minute to decide whether to abandon her attempt and jump sideways out of the wheel, and was just contemplating how to do that without bashing her head on the stockroom shelves when...

The spokes started glowing. She couldn't look directly at them without getting dangerously dizzy, but could definitely sense an eerie brightening in the air around her head. Then, almost immediately, the light kicked into gear properly, the siren started wailing, and with her heart threatening to leap out of her chest with a mixture of fear, excitement, and exertion, she made a swift, silent wish against all sense that she wasn't about to do herself a terrible injury, and tried to do just as she'd seen Mr Pitts do. She leapt up into the air, grabbing her nose, and...

She was gone.

The Underwhere

The next few moments were eerily calm. Millie wasn't moving, as far as she could tell, neither was she standing on, sitting on, hanging from, or touching anything at all. Everything around her was completely black, but a blackness that felt as though it had depth to it as well as colour. Three-dimensional black. And her surroundings were completely silent, like when you're going on holiday and you've eaten all your boiled sweets while your plane's still on the runway, and end up with blocked ears when it takes off.

Millie was certain she was dead. She was really fed up about this. She was usually quite a good learner, particularly when it came to physical things, so she'd have been shouting out a whopping great "Oh POO-

POO-POO-POO-POO!" to herself even if she'd only slightly damaged herself by scraping her knee getting on the wheel or something. But actually dying, even though she'd done everything exactly as her rather vague, very weird instructor had suggested, felt really, really unfair.

"POPPING POO PANCAKES!! AAAAAARGH...." She wailed.

Then suddenly (again, just like on a plane) her ears popped, and she could hear a quiet whooshing sound all around her. The rest of her senses had been unlocked, too, as she could soon feel the air rushing up from beneath her, smelling richly of earth and leaving a metallic taste on her tongue. What's more, she could begin to see sparkling crystal-like flecks whizzing past her, which she realised must be dotted along the inside of the walls of what could only be... the tunnel! She'd made it through the floor of the wheel and into the Underwhere!

The fact that she wasn't dead made Millie very happy indeed. But this happiness was short-lived, as she soon became very aware of the fact that she was currently flying through the inside of the earth at terrifying speed towards who-knew-where, facing completely unknown dangers with only a toothbrush for protection. Where on earth – or rather where *in* earth – was she heading?

The answer was about to arrive, with a bump.

The Plains

J ust as she'd got used to the sensation of flying through the tunnel, the whooshing noise grew to a crazy crescendo, the glittery crystals rushed towards her feet in bigger, brighter groups, and the atmosphere around her started to feel less damp and cool. Suddenly, like a cork popping out of a champagne bottle, Millie erupted back into the world in a burst of light. She felt her feet slam into solid ground, and after a brief judder all was peaceful and silent again, until…

"DUCK, MARY!"

It was a good thing that Millie had got used to Mr Pitts' random name calling now, as otherwise she'd have almost certainly been decapitated. Her head would've been knocked cleanly off her shoulders by the tree branch springing towards her at devastating speed had she not dropped like a stone to the ground, squishing her face into it. And what a strange, unfamiliar sort of ground it was! Rather than the musty, metallic soil she'd just been whizzing through, this was a black, clay-like texture with chips of stone in it. Most unusual of all, though, was the fact that it was warm. As was the back of her head. And the back of her legs. The sun was beating down on her with such strength that even from her earthward-facing position it was clear to Millie that she was *not* in Harpleford any more. She turned her head gingerly to one side and spotted Mr Pitts sitting cross-legged on top of a small rock, smiling sheepishly at her. He held his toothbrush in one hand, and some sort of pine cone in another.

"I'm terribly sorry," he said. "I dropped down in a slightly skew-whiff manner, grabbed an armful of tree as I fell over, at which point this (he waved the cone) detached itself from the rest of the branch, which pinged back and, well, nearly did you quite a serious mischief. Are you okay?"

"I'm fine", Millie replied, standing up and dusting herself off. "Just a bit dizzy."

Utterly bamboozled and freaking out at the craziness of this situation more like, she was actually thinking, but she was determined to keep up her reputation as a fearless explorer and as such, had to at least pretend to be taking it all in her stride. *Fake it 'til you make it, Mills,* she told herself, repeating a phrase she'd heard on one of the television talent shows her Mum sometimes insisted they all watch together as a family.

She took a moment to survey her surroundings. She was standing next to a short, spindly tree perched on top of a rocky hilltop. The view to her right was stunted by a line of much more lush vegetation on a ridge in the distance, but as she turned her head to the left, she was rewarded by the sight of a vast, grassy plain that stretched out below as far as she could see and shimmered in the heat of a baking sun. There wasn't a cloud in the sky, and as her eyes adjusted to the light, she began to be able to focus on clumps of movement in the distance that looked like packs of animals of some sort.

Hopefully Mr Pitts would be able to explain where exactly they were, as well as providing the answers to a few other, urgent, questions.

"You know the gigantic hamster wheel that catapulted us here in the first place? Well, why isn't there one at this end? And how are we going to get back home from here? And where exactly is here, anyway?"

"More very good questions, Millhouse! I knew you had a clever brain in that head of yours – I'm so relieved it's still attached to your shoulders.

"One of the many interesting things about sub-soil transference is that all the hard work is done on the outbound journey; the return leg is simple, which is why we don't have to worry about the transfer window on the way back. Your Rotatormate, or equivalent transportation machine, generates a huge amount of energy that forces you into and along the sub-soil pathway. But as you fly along it, you trail a sort of invisible rubber band that stretches out behind you as you go. This helps the traveller slow down as they approach their destination, and hooks itself to a sturdy point in the landing zone – in our case, here." At this, Mr Pitts tapped the rock he was sitting on. "This is mine, and that is yours." He pointed to the tree nearest to Millie, and she had to admit it did look a little wonkier than its neighbours. "When we want to go back, all we have to do is jump into the drop-down zone and *whump* – we'll be on our way home."

This all sounded bonkers to Millie, but then she *had* burrowed her way to the other side of the world in seconds by running on a human-sized hamster wheel this morning, so perhaps she needed to rethink her definition of what 'bonkers' meant.

"As for the question of where we are, well, we're on the Namiri plains of the Serengeti National Park in Africa – the name means 'Big Cat' in Swahili. It's one of the most beautiful natural environments in the world, habitat to hundreds of amazing species of animal, route of amazing migrations, and, unless the Society of Extraordinary Adventurers manages to save it, the future graveyard of almost every one of the millions of creatures that calls it home …"

Trooper's Plan

raveyard? Millions of creatures? Millie's heart stopped. She hadn't even had a chance to get used to the beauty of the landscape that surrounded her yet, let alone to the idea that so many incredible animals were roaming around within sight of her very own eyes, and Mr Pitts was now suggesting that they could be gone, *forever*? She choked back her breath and turned to face him. He may have been an oddball, but Mr Pitts could clearly recognise a distressed child when he saw one, as his tone softened, and he continued.

"It's probably best if I explain a little more about this place. You see, the Serengeti grasslands have been here since the very beginning of the world as we know it, forming millions of years ago when the first great ice age was melting away and animal life was starting to flourish on the planet. It stretches between Tanzania to the south and west, and to Kenya in the north and east. It covers an area of twelve thousand square miles, and as well as playing host to two million humans it's home to nearly a thousand different species of animal, countless numbers of which travel across it in huge groups every spring and summer as they migrate to the north. It's quite rightly thought of as one of the seven great wonders of the ancient world. But the modern world might just be about to kill it."

Mr Pitts paused, and cast his eyes towards the distant treeline.

"Over there," he nodded his head towards them, "is a valley in which sits the secret research base for Sun Flash – the most selfish, arrogant, evil corporation to have ever existed. A company that operates purely to make as much money as it can. A company that doesn't care that in order to achieve this aim it will put an end to hundreds of species that have lived on this planet for longer than anyone alive today can fathom. A company that cares so little for the future it sees nothing wrong with turning children into sleep-deprived robots in pursuit of a one in a billion chance of winning riches that they won't even be able to spend, as there'll be no planet left to spend their money on by the time they're grown-up."

"This *organisation*," he spat the word out, "has been testing something that in other hands could have helped save this poor, dying planet of ours." (Here, he slapped the rock he was sitting on as though it were a faithful dog who was getting on a bit). "You see, the Serengeti gets a huge amount of sunlight, as it sits right on the equator. What Sun Flash has managed to do is work out a way to capture the energy of the sun to create solar power at a scale that's never been achieved before; enough to keep every one of the millions of Flash Pack consoles it's about to unleash upon the world fully charged at all times.

"Now, if this power were being harvested in a way that didn't impact on the environment around it, the technology would be a great thing, of course. But in order to generate the vast amount of energy needed to power its Flash Packs, the company needs to use every square metre of land you can see around you here to install huge solar panels. It's told the authorities in charge of protecting the savannah that its work is limited to the valley beyond the treeline but we at the Society know better – Sun Flash is planning a sudden assault on the whole plain, carving up the habitat of our animal friends and replacing it with slabs of metal and glass the size of football pitches in a matter of hours, to feed its evil ambitions before anyone can do anything about it. By the time anyone can intervene, the world will be addicted to *Trooper's Treasure Tunnel* and nobody will care about this beautiful land any more.

Mr Pitts paused, and the anger that had been apparent in his features was replaced by a look of deep sorrow.

"As if this wasn't going to be devastating enough for the wildlife that needs this land for the food and water it provides, there's an even more unforgiveable side effect to the Sun Flash business plan. The equipment the company plans to use is extremely delicate in places, and certainly wouldn't work particularly well if it were trampled by, say, a herd of migrating Wildebeest. So, all the way along the borders of the solar farm it's going to dig huge ditches, many metres deep and filled with rocks and boulders that will break the bones of every poor animal that falls into it. If our suspicions about Sun Flash are correct, they're going to try to force any animal of any species that comes near into those ditches. It's just too awful to…"

Mr Pitts stopped; his voice thick with tears. Millie gave him a moment to compose himself before asking some of the questions that were rattling around in her mind.

"I know all about Sun Flash – my brother Josh is obsessed with them and Jeremiah Trooper even came to our school last week. But how do you know so much about it and its plan? And why can't you just tell the world about what's going on? And what can we do to stop it?"

"Here you are with the questions again, eh, Marjorie?" Mr Pitts replied, kindly. "Well, one of the Society's members managed to infiltrate the company a few months ago and they're now working there, doing their pretend job quite badly I hasten to add, as one of our Members Operating Largely in Extreme Secrecy, or MOLES for short. They've been feeding secret intelligence out to us by carrier hippo.

"But telling the world about the plan is much, much harder to achieve. You see, an awful lot of people on this planet are a bit selfish and short-sighted by nature, and unless they see something happening right in front of them that's affecting their daily life in a bad way, they'll simply ignore it. That's why our governments don't bother getting involved either; they focus on the things that make them popular at home. And the Society knows from painful experience that if we try to expose wrong-doing without being absolutely certain we'll win the battle, we'll be drowned out by the weight of the noise the sort of powerful, wealthy people we're always up against can make.

"As for stopping it, well, we're trying very hard to come up with a plan, but the best idea we've got involves recruiting an exceptional individual with a very specific talent, and we've not been able to find them. Yet." At this, he raised an eyebrow ever so slightly in Millie's direction, making her heart beat just a tiny bit faster and her breath come just a tiny bit more quickly. He couldn't mean she might be this special recruit, could he?

She was about to quiz him further, but they were very suddenly and very rudely interrupted by a lion, and their conversation had to be put on hold for a bit.

The Pride

The thing about lions, Millie thought later, is that it's actually completely understandable that they get cross from time to time. Take the scenario that was unfolding now, for instance. Imagine if you'd been playing in the den you'd carefully constructed in your back garden for the last month then came back from the shops to find that a couple of, say, geese had invaded it and were sitting there, merrily honking away at each other, you'd probably be quite put out about the situation. Well this was a bit like that. Only instead of people there were lions. And instead of geese there were Millie and Mr Pitts.

Just as their conversation was getting particularly interesting, and just as Millie thought she was about to learn about some wonderful gift she possessed that could help to save the world, Mr Pitts paused, and held his hand up towards her in a way that made it abundantly clear she should at this moment keep very, very still and very, very quiet. A scraping, scratching sound was emerging from behind one of the boulders on the hillside below them, like a garden rake being dragged across a patio. This scrabbling noise grew louder and more insistent, before suddenly a pair of paws the size of dinner plates appeared on top of the rock, swiftly followed by a mane of fur that blocked out the sun behind it, encircling the beautiful but terrifying face of an African lion. As he settled his immense haunches on the rock, two lionesses appeared around either side of it on the ground below – ears pricked, eyes focused on the humans, ready for an unknown signal that could nevertheless mean big, bad trouble. They'd clearly been here many times before. In fact, Millie got the distinct impression this whole hilltop was their home, and that she and Mr Pitts were probably trespassing in their living room.

The lion turned his head from side to side, sizing up the humans. There was menace in his steely eyes, for sure, but not fury. It was more a look that suggested annoyance, with a hint of interest, than anything else, for now. He turned his head towards Mr Pitts (who had frozen his face so completely he was doing an incredibly good impression of one of the human statues Millie had seen in the town centre from time to time), then slowly tilted his head until his gaze rested on her. It was at this point that she started to rethink her ambition to be an adventurer and decided it might be better to work in a bank after all; her legs trembled, her stomach flipped, and it took every last ounce of willpower in her body to keep looking at the beast.

Things could've turned out very differently had these few seconds not played out in this manner. Millie might have been eaten, Mr Pitts might have been eaten, or at the very least someone would have lost a digit or two. But after a few seconds of staring at the great animal, something quite remarkable happened. While she was looking at him, Millie found herself falling into a sort of trance, and, possibly because of the incredible things that had already happened to her today, or perhaps because she simply had nothing to lose, she decided to find out where that trance might lead. She opened her eyes a bit wider, took a deep breath through her nose, and began silently addressing the lion:

Hello there, Mr Lion. I mean sir, er, your honour, your highness, your graceship, your magnificence. Sorry, I've not done this before, so I don't really know what to call you. But I do know you totally deserve your 'King of Beasts' nickname. You look fully awesome, and I'm not just saying or, er, thinking so because you're standing on a rock in front of me. I appreciate you're probably a bit put out about a pair of strangers turning up at your home uninvited, especially when I'm guessing the only experience you've had with humans recently is of them tearing up your neighbourhood. But I'd be really, really grateful if you could believe me when I say, sorry, er, think, that my friend and I are here to help. You see, I don't quite know exactly how *I got here, but I know* why *I got here, which is because my friend and I love our fellow creatures dearly – not just you and your pride but the other animals that you share the Serengeti with. And we care deeply about the land you live on and your future, and we're only here because we want to put a stop to…*

At this point her train of thought-speech was cut short by the sight of the lion, who'd been holding her gaze this whole time, opening his great mouth, exposing two rows of enormous dagger-sharp teeth, and letting out a roar so deep and powerful that it threatened to shake the huge boulders out of the earth and send them tumbling down the hillside. Strangely, this didn't unsettle Millie. She had a sense it was an acknowledgement, or at the very least an understanding, of what she'd said. This feeling was heightened when, instead of deciding to make a light supper of her and Mr Pitts, he turned his back on them, dropped down off the rock, and padded away out of sight, with the lionesses following behind. In that moment, for some unknown but incredibly thrilling reason, she was certain that the message had got across, and that she'd made an ally.

Millie turned to Mr Pitts just as he snapped himself out of his statue-like stillness. He was looking at her intently, his forehead shiny with sweat but his eyes bright with excitement.

"You've *got* it, Millie!" he stage-whispered, plainly terrified of attracting the lion's attention and reminding him that although the female human was now a buddy, the male might still be worth a bit of a chew. "I was right! You're a CATASTROPHE!"

"A what?" Millie asked. She thought she'd done quite well saving their lives, and the fact Mr Pitts was using her name correctly for once ought to have been encouraging. But it sounded a lot like he telling her she was a disaster.

"A Catastrophe!" he beamed, "A big cat conversationalist! A cheetah chatterer, a jaguar jabberer! Think of any feline you can name, and you can talk to it! I was right, you're just what we need!

"The S.E.A is a small organisation in human terms – it has to be in order to protect its subsoil secrets from exploitation by less earth-friendly types – so we have to enlist the help of our animal friends from time to time. And to do *that*, we need to recruit people who can communicate with them using their minds. We have Waverers who talk to whales, Architects who speak to arachnids, even Boverers – they communicate with bovines. Some of them just help out occasionally, while others become full-time members of the Society along the way. I'd love to tell you more about them , but if it's all the same to you I'd rather not risk sticking around and would quite like us to go home now. That sound okay?"

Millie nodded.

"Good. Now, remember what I said about the return leg, or the downside-up leg as I prefer to call it – just jump into the drop-down zone and you'll snap yourself back to the shop. Don't forget to hold your nose, and you'll be fine. Although do be prepared for a little bit of flatulence when you land. You'll have noticed it's a few hours later in the day here, on account of the time zone difference, and when you jump back the experience tends to squeeze the hours you missed back out through your bottom, for some reason. Still, at least you don't have to worry about the toothbrush in this direction!"

Millie was hardly reassured by the fact she didn't have to hold on to a small plastic stick on her way back given that she was still going to be hurtling through the underside of the earth at hundreds of miles a second, but she didn't get a chance to raise this point with him. She had just enough time to sweep an exotic-looking feather from the ground beneath her and stuff it into her pocket (*that's number 363!* she thought triumphantly), before Mr Pitts had jumped off his rock, shoved Millie over to a patch of ground beneath the wonky tree, given it an almighty shove, and the whole world turned sideways as she felt herself being yanked back into the earth beneath her.

Downside-Up

The return leg was just as brain-boggling as the outward journey for Millie as she hurtled back through the sub-soil, not least because she was moving head-first this time, and if she had to bash into something she'd always found it preferable to do so with her feet rather than with her head. She still sensed the metallic taste of the air, the flashing brightness of the tunnel walls, and the whooshing noise around her, but at least this was less unfamiliar to her now. *If it wasn't for the fact that I might headbutt a badger at any moment I might actually enjoy this experience*, she thought.

She most certainly did not enjoy the landing.

Hurtling up through the opening in the shop floor,

Millie burst between the slats of the hamster wheel and found herself flattened around the inside top edge of it, staring back down through the slats at the bottom towards the hole in the floor beneath her. With a creak and a judder, the wheel swung itself around under the weight of its new passenger, and rocked Millie back down to the ground like a swing with nobody pushing it, until she was curled up on her back, facing the roof of the shop.

It was at this point that she farted.

Her Mum very primly called them 'pops', but in this case, there really was no other word for what emerged from Millie's backside than a fart, and a tremendous, bum-shaking, deafening monster of a fart at that. The booming raspberry shook the filing cabinet that leaned against the wall, made the shelves quiver, and rattled the wood beneath Millie's bottom so violently that the whole experience nearly propelled her up and out of the wheel altogether. She giggled, a little embarrassed, but also rather proud of her creation, and stood up just in time to see Mr Pitts explode through the floor himself, rocking to a standstill in the same way she had, and letting rip with an even greater butt-bomb than she'd managed. He leapt up, looked her up and down as though checking a bike for damage after a particularly adventurous cycle ride, and nodded to himself.

"Good. Limbs intact, face unsquashed, no

screaming noises... I think we can pronounce your first sub-soil round trip a success, Martin!"

"Thanks, Mr Pitts. I actually quite enjoyed it."

"Of course you did! You're an adventurer! This is what we live for!"

"Now, as you'll be aware, we've got a lot to get on with if we're going to stop Jeremiah Trooper and Sun Flash destroying the savannah. And we don't have a lot of time in which to do it. However, we can't go drawing attention to ourselves, so, I need you to head home and go about your usual routine as if absolutely nothing out of the ordinary is going on in your life. I'll do a bit of bouncing back and forth between zones to lay the groundwork – don't worry, I won't be putting myself in the path of any more dangerous animals – then if you come back here next Saturday in time for the 09:00 transfer window, we'll be able to start putting our plan into action in plenty of time to scupper the game launch."

Millie wanted to point out that Mr Pitts hadn't actually outlined his plan to her yet but didn't get a chance, as he waved her out of the door of the shop and back into the blinking sunlight of Harpleford High Street. The next week was going to be a long one.

Grounded

"You did *WHAT*?"

Millie's Mum was not happy with her daughter. In fact, it would be a lot more accurate to say she was exceptionally unhappy with her. It had all started with Josh, as was often the case when she ended up in trouble. He'd been heading back home on the bus from town ahead of his parents, having stocked up on energy drinks and been eager to get in some more game practice, and had spotted Millie being ushered out of Criceta's Emporium with a dazed look on her face. He'd wasted no time asking her, very loudly, what she'd been doing in the strange (he called it freaky) little shop with the peculiar (he called *him* freaky) little man over dinner that evening, which tonight consisted of congealed lumps of what might once have been individual strands of spaghetti, topped with a mush of gristly mince and watery tomato sauce. Her parents had, predictably, been far from amused to hear about Millie's visit to what in their eyes was a highly sinister-looking establishment, and had been even less impressed when she'd cracked under the pressure of their interrogation. She'd blurted out that she'd met an amazing fellow adventurer and that she was going to help him save the Serengeti before realising her mistake and buttoning her lip. But she'd already said enough for her Mum to see red.

"How many times do I have to tell you that 'adventuring' is not an appropriate interest for a girl of your age, or any age for that matter? It's not going to put food on your table, it's not going to make you friends, and it's not going to be of interest to any responsible mortgage lender! And as for consorting with odd little men on Harpleford High Street, I really shouldn't have to tell you how humiliating it would be if you were spotted in such strange company by any of our friends, or (she clutched her chest for dramatic effect) *Dorian*. You deal with her, Maurice - I'm off for a lie down." With that, her Mum shot up from her dining chair and stormed out of the room.

Her Dad, who could always be relied upon to take

a slightly more sympathetic position any time she was being told off, looked at her sadly.

"I know you love your stories, Mills, and believe me, I know how it feels to want to embark on a grand adventure, but your Mum's right – it's not going to get you anywhere. I don't know whether this Mr Pitts is just a bit wobbly in the head, or if he's some sort of con artist, but I'm going to have words with him and tell him to leave off involving my daughter in this nonsense. And I'm afraid I'm going to have to ground you, too. For the whole of this week, you're going to come straight back home from school and go straight up to your room. Maybe you could get on the line on your computer, explore the world that way?"

Millie knew there was no point arguing with her Dad over this; although he could be persuaded to give in to some of her requests, the prospect of a tongue-lashing from his wife trumped any chance of him going soft on Millie. "It's online, dad, not on the line", she said, quietly, and got up from the table.

As she left the room to go upstairs her attention was drawn to an advert playing on the television in the lounge. 'IMPORTANT NEWS COMING! STAY RIGHT WHERE YOU ARE!' screamed a message in bright red text, flashing on the screen. Josh, who until then had been smirking into his tablet at the table, nearly rugby-tackled her out of the way in his haste to get to the sofa to watch. The perfectly circular, pink-hued head of that awful man Trooper filled the screen, speaking directly to his viewers:

"Hey you! Yes, YOU! It's me – Jeremiah Trooper – here to tell you some VERY IMPORTANT, LIFE-CHANGING news! As a result of my business brilliance and my technological terrificness we're going to be able to launch our EARTH-SHATTERING new game TROOPER'S TREASURE TUNNEL even sooner than we'd thought! We no longer have to wait until the end of the month, but can get started on DAY ONE of your school summer break. Yes, that's right, you now have just 10 days to get your gaming fingers in gear, make sure you're packing some additional energy reserves (here he patted his obscene belly as it wobbled with excitement), and tell your family you won't be going on holiday with them after all, as we at Sun Flash are ALL SET to unleash upon the world the greatest, richest, most talked about and most fiendishly addictive game you will ever have the privilege of playing!"

The camera zoomed out to show him standing in the middle of an enormous warehouse filled with teenagers, some lounging on beanbags, others at bar stools set around high-topped tables, and every single one of them glued to some sort of gaming tablet. Along the entire length of one wall, a timer was projecting the time until launch, next Saturday at

11.59pm UK time. The whole scene looked like a warped battery farm to Millie, with children where the poor chickens would usually be crammed, but Trooper was in his element.

"These guys are getting their practice in, folks!" he continued, getting more and more excited, "but don't worry, they're just our testers so won't have a chance to win the prize. But just in case you've been in a coma for the last six weeks, let me remind you exactly what that prize is… (he was screeching now) IT'S ONE. TRILLION. DOLLARS!"

At this, the warehouse was replaced on screen by the explosion of dollar bills that had previously been used at the school presentation, accompanied by a soundtrack of whooping, whistling, and cheering. Suddenly the camera cut back to the close-up of Trooper's face, now deadly serious.

"We'll be seeing you soon folks. And who knows how long we're going to spend together before the prize is claimed? Oh, and you might as well tell your parents to ditch these, too, (he pretended to tap the inside of the television screen). Where we're going, you won't be needing Tee Vee anymore." With a final wink, the advert ended.

The man's completely crazy, Millie thought. *And if I don't stop him within the next ten days, he's going to destroy us all.*

The Amazing Mo

The experience of being grounded is not a pleasant one for any child. But for a child who needs to feel the air on their face and the earth beneath their feet in order to be truly alive it's worse than any other punishment you can imagine. (Yes, even being told you can never have another ice cream in your life. No, not even one of those boring plain vanilla ones without any sprinkles or flake in a cone that tastes of cardboard). So by the end of Millie's first 24 hours under house arrest she was tearing at her curly hair with frustration. Her exasperation was made even more intense as a result of the rapid acceleration of the launch of *Trooper's Treasure Tunnel*, and the fact that whatever plan Mr

Pitts had in store to stop it was going to have to happen in half the time he'd planned.

She was determined to break free from her grounding when the school week got back underway and sneak off to warn him (she was pretty sure he didn't have a TV), but for the rest of the weekend her parents co-ordinated their arrangements in order that one of them would always be around to keep an eye on her. They were extra-cautious about this, and with good reason. During a previous house arrest Millie had attempted to escape via her bedroom window and ended up dangling by her legs from a tree that grew tantalisingly close to the house (her Mum had dropped and smashed one of her favourite casserole dishes when her daughter's upside down face had suddenly swung into view through the patio doors below). The upstairs windows in the house had immediately all been fitted with locks for precisely this sort of situation.

However, the fact that the upper floor of the house was so secure also meant that her parents didn't bother going up to check on her whereabouts very often. So Millie was able to roam around undisturbed.

On Sunday morning, once the family's 'special' breakfast of gloopy scrambled eggs dolloped on to toast that was somehow both soggy and burnt at the same time had been consumed, Millie's mum headed out for her weekly Sunday morning park run and her

Dad settled down in the living room with the papers. Josh didn't even bother leaving the dining room; he simply grabbed the tablet that had been sitting on his lap throughout the meal, rested his elbows on the table, and was immediately tuned out from everything else going on around him.

Millie, meanwhile, took the opportunity to have a poke around in her parents' spare bedroom, or 'the guest suite' as her mum insisted on calling it just because she'd left a travel kettle, some teabags and a carton of long-life milk on top of the drawers.

One corner of the room housed a built-in wardrobe, in which her Dad's supermarket overalls usually hung. Behind the wardrobe rail sat half a dozen storage shelves. The cupboard was deep enough to need a light, but the bulb in it had burned out a long time ago, so any belongings on the shelves were hidden in the darkness, forgotten about by everyone except Millie, who decided to explore the boxes they contained.

Millie lifted the boxes from the shelves one by one, rifling through the contents in search of something interesting. But all she found was old paperwork: bills, out of date passports, stacks of birthday cards, and long-forgotten catalogues and junk mail. Just as she was about to give up on her investigation, she caught sight of a box that looked slightly different to the others, buried right at the back of the bottom shelf.

She reached in and pulled it out. It was made of tin, for a start. For another thing, it was much larger – about the size of the carry-on suitcases that her parents made them squeeze all their holiday clothes into to avoid paying airline luggage fees. Its side panels were covered in faded yellow paint, rust clung to its edges, and the lid showed an illustration that Millie couldn't quite make out under a thick layer of dust. She wiped her sleeve across the surface to clean it. The picture showed a circus tent, its flaps open to reveal three figures: a fire-breather, a juggler, and a sword-swallower.

Millie grabbed the edges of the tin and gingerly lifted the lid. Lying on a bed of tissue paper stretching diagonally from one corner of the box to the other was a gleaming silver sword, with a blade as wide as Millie's thumb was long, and an intricate black handle in the shape of a twisting snake. She carefully lifted it out, taking the tissue paper with it. Further down lay a jumble of material which Millie unfolded, revealing a pair of black trousers with silver braces attached to the waist, along with a billowy shirt with a wide, open neck. Next came a bowler hat, with a square of card sticking out of the rim on which the words 'THANK YOU!' were written in a dramatic scrawl. Below that came a bundle of papers held together with a rubber band. Millie peeled one sheet off and held it up to the light. Inside a hand-drawn border of multi-coloured stars, exclamation points and questions marks was an invitation printed in bold red lettering:

'Come and witness the most trepidatious, tantalising, sensational sword-swallowing show on the planet! Watch THE AMAZING MO perform feats of extraordinary daredevildom, sending the SHARPEST STEEL SPIKES you've ever seen THROUGH his THROAT to the BOTTOM of his BELLY. Without trickery, without tomfoolery, and without a tea break! Prepare to be definitively dazzled! (every Saturday, Harpleford town square, 11am. Donations gratefully received).'

"What are you doing, Mills?"

Millie had been so engrossed in her discovery that she'd failed to notice her Dad's footsteps as he came upstairs to check on her. She turned, dropping the flyer she was holding, and it floated slowly to the floor. He picked it up with a sad smile.

"So you've discovered my secret past, eh, darling? Don't worry, Nan told me she might have let the cat out of the bag a bit about my experiences with the sharp arts" – he nodded to the blade – "and the sorry conclusion to that particular adventure."

He perched on the end of the spare room bed and continued.

"Does this make it easier for you to understand why me and your Mum get nervous when we hear you talking about how you want a life filled with adventure? Adventure goes hand in hand with risks and danger, Mills, and even if we don't always show it, we think you're far too precious to do anything that puts you in harm's way. And besides," he joked, "I'm not convinced Joshie's going to make us all millionaires with his career path; we'll need you healthy so you can support us in our old age. You know I don't mind you tearing around outside from time to time, but just promise you won't put yourself in any danger, will you?"

Millie paused, as she contemplated the lie she was about to tell. She took a deep breath.

"Okay, Dad. I promise."

He reached down and gave her chin a little tweak before kissing the top of her head.

"Thanks, Mills. Now why don't you put this lot back where it belongs while I go and make us both a cup of double-strength hot chocolate. With marshmallows."

A Dressing-Down

Thankfully, Millie didn't have to wait too long before she was able to put her escape plan into action. Her Mum's bank was holding its annual summer quiz night on Wednesday, and as branch manager she had to attend, while her Dad was working a late shift at the supermarket and wouldn't be home until after 10. Technically, Josh was in charge of keeping an eye on Millie's movements, but he was shut away in his bedroom, so obsessed with making himself 'match fit' for the launch of Trooper's Treasure Tunnel that she could have invited a herd of elephants for a karaoke party in the living room without him noticing. She returned home from school with him, watched him tear up to his room and shut himself in, grabbed her toothbrush from the bathroom, and hurried straight out again to Criceta's Emporium.

Before she had a chance to deliver her update, though, Mr Pitts let rip at her.

"What part of the phrase 'this is a secret organisation so don't tell anyone about it' didn't you understand, Millicent? I had your father in here on Saturday afternoon complaining that I'd been encouraging irresponsible behaviour and that I should knock it off before he called the council! For some unfathomable reason he seems to think my premises are unhygienic and is threatening to get me shut down!

"And where would that leave us? And the poor creatures of the savannah? You know exactly where – it'd leave them homeless at best, or dead in a ditch at worst, and it'd leave us living in a dying world full of videogame-playing zombie children. If it weren't for your Catastrophic gifts I'd be ending our business together right this very moment!

"Anyway, I thought you were meant to be grounded – what are you doing here?" He'd stopped shouting now, unable to contain his curiosity and finding himself just a little bit impressed with Millie's resourcefulness.

"My brother's in charge and he's an idiot. And I'm sorry for telling my parents about you. But this is all so important, Mr Pitts."

"Well okay, I can see why one might be unable to fight one's urges to tell the world about the impending doom about to befall it. But as I told you before, we know from painful experience that corporations like Sun Flash can drown us out in a moment with a slick announcement accusing us of being scaremongers or criminals. It doesn't even have to be true as long as they shout it loud enough."

"I understand, Mr Pitts, I really do, but I'm at the end of my tether to be honest. And our mission just got harder I'm afraid – it's what I came here to warn you about. Sun Flash has brought the launch of its console forward to this weekend. We only have a few days to stop them."

There was a small squeak, then Mr Pitts disappeared from behind the till as he fainted.

Into Action

Mr Pitts sprang back up just as quickly as he'd dropped to the floor in the first place, and started talking as though the whole fainting thing had never happened. He seemed (to Millie's non-medically trained eyes) to have completely lost the plot.

"So it's obviously a biiiiiiiit of a setback but it's nothing we can't cope with of course and as long as your, er, skills don't let us down I see no reason why a 12 year-old schoolgirl who's only visited the Serengeti once – and fleetingly at that – shouldn't be able to scupper the plans of one of the world's biggest and most dangerous corporations. And yessssss, they may have employed a hundred 6 foot tall guards trained in martial arts and other horrible skills whose only job is to prevent meddlers like us meddling at all costs – using extreme force if necessary – but we've got a 5 foot tall girl who may or may not have once demonstrated the telepathic ability to prevent a pride of lions eating her and her slightly less than 5 foot tall companion. So, who's got the better chances, eh? You'd have to say it's extremely hard to call!"

Millie would not have to say this at all. And she could see plenty of reasons why she and Mr Pitts wouldn't be able to do anything to stop the might of Jeremiah Trooper and his Sun Flash employees getting away with their despicable plan. But it was clear that Mr Pitts was deadly serious in his assessment of the situation, as he headed off through the curtain into the storeroom, evidently assuming she would be following him through.

"So, if we've got four days instead of ten, we'll just have to speed up the whole shindig: recce today, prep tomorrow and Friday, and D-day Saturday. And we're about to hit today's 16:00 window! There's not a moment to lose, Minimum!"

Millie didn't have a clue what most of this meant, but it was clear Mr Pitts had a plan in mind, so she decided her best course of action was to simply do as she was told, for now. She followed him back into the storeroom where the giant hamster wheel stood waiting for them, pulling her toothbrush out of her back pocket in readiness for the trip.

"Ha! Toothbrush at the ready I see! That's another

tick on the old Society application form for you – preparedness under any circumstance. You're looking a definite maybe to be offered membership at the end of all of this, Mincemeat.

"We'll need a few more supplies this time. Here, grab one of these."

Mr Pitts threw an old canvas backpack over to Millie, and grabbed another for himself. Hers was quite light, but made a clanking sound as she put it on. He beckoned to her.

"You go first this time; you know the drill. Just stay perfectly still when you land, and I'll be along right behind you."

Millie felt a little self-conscious as she stepped up and into the wheel, but her embarrassment swiftly vanished as her attention turned instead to getting the giant contraption into motion. One step, then two, then three… the familiar creaking and clattering noises of the machine and the groaning from the ground beneath it faded into the background as her eyes focused on the clock in front of her and her concentration fixed on getting the wheel up to speed. Out of the corner of her eye she noticed the light on the metal box on the middle of the frame flashing, then almost immediately, she heard the siren. She slapped one hand over her nose, made sure her other was firmly gripping the toothbrush, and jumped.

The subsoil experience was slightly less discombobulating this time around and Millie actually found herself able to pay a little more attention to what was going on around her. This time, she noticed not only the glittering mineral-studded rocks flashing past, but also what looked like signs of life. Was that the front end (or rear?) of a worm poking out of the earthy wall? A mole's tail? And did she perhaps see the snout of a fox popping into the tunnel as she whizzed past? She found herself enjoying the experience, marvelling at whatever magical power was enabling her to embark on such an incredible journey.

She was knocked out of her daydream by a rather large bump on her rather delicate bottom. Instead of landing on the grassy patch she'd hit on her previous journey, Millie had landed on the rock that Mr Pitts had been sitting on when she'd taken her first trip, winding herself in the process. Of course, she realised, the transference pathways or whatever they were called must deposit their passengers in some sort of order to stop them squashing each other; the rock was always the first landing spot, the tree was the second. But that realisation didn't make it any less painful. As she struggled to get the air back into her lungs, she made a mental note to ask Mr Pitts for a bit more clarity about these things from now on.

She was relieved to see that there weren't any disgruntled lions lying around – yet – so was able to pocket her toothbrush before gingerly easing herself off the rock and looking around. The last rays of sun stretched out across the landscape, casting long shadows beyond everything they touched and making the whole sight even more beautiful than it had been on her last trip. This made Millie even angrier at the thought of its impending destruction, and even more determined to put a stop to it. She stepped slowly across the clearing, and then…

Whump!

Mr Pitts careered into the ground in front of her, head-first, with a rucksack almost the same size as him strapped to his back. The weight of the pack must have tipped him upside down during his journey. He balanced in a handstand position for a moment, then toppled face down onto the ground, squashed underneath his oversized luggage.

"Grphh hrmm plcchbk…" he mumbled. "Glumpph prlch bummgll!"

Millie's communication skills evidently translated beyond animals to 'people with a mouthful of earth' as she realised he was asking her to grab the backpack. She grasped it firmly in both hands, and heaved it off Mr Pitts' shoulders. He staggered to his feet, spitting out a big wet ball of clay.

"Thank you," he said, looking more than a little embarrassed. No wonder, thought Millie, he was meant to be the expert at this business after all.

Mr Pitts opened his pack and pulled out unfolded what looked like a music stand with a small umbrella perched on top. He carried this over to the tree that had nearly taken her head off on their last visit and stood it up next to the trunk, where it would be well hidden.

"This," he said, "is our Mapping Module. It'll help us work out exactly where we need to be when it gets dark. And in order to use it, we also have to have these…"

He returned to his pack and rustled around in it again. He pulled out a brown apple core, an old copy of *Rodent Weekly* magazine, a tape measure, and some toenail clippers before picking out a thick rubber disc the size of a dinner plate, with small bobbles protruding all around its edge. He paused to press a few buttons on one of its flatter sides, then gave it to Millie.

"What you're holding in your hands now, Mildew, is a Bumpass. It's like a compass, but instead of a dial to show you the way, the bumps around the edge expand in the direction you need to go – as long as you've programmed it correctly."

"As for these…" he continued, reaching back into his sack again, "they're going to be useful if we need a little assistance from our feline friends."

Mr Pitts was now holding a small metal stick about the same size of one of Millie's school rulers, with a spike at one end, and a golf-ball sized sphere at the other, wrapped in greasy brown paper.

"What you're looking at here is a Pathwinder. You wedge the sharp end in the ground, and when you're ready to activate the guidance system you simply rip the paper off and wait for the cavalry to arrive. Although there aren't any horses in these parts so it's more likely to be something rather more exotic. These balls contain a powerful scent that's undetectable to humans but phenomenally attractive to big cats."

"Like catnip, you mean?"

"Sort of, although the cats around here aren't quite so much fun to play with. Anyway, they can smell a Pathwinder from miles upon miles away, and come flocking to it out of sheer inquisitiveness. When they reach it, you just need a plan to get them to do what you want. Which is where a Catastrophe comes in, of course.

"Now, follow me. We'd better get ourselves down there," he waved towards the line of trees that marked the border of the Sun Flash research facility, "and figure out our new plan."

Once again, Millie's head was spinning. She tried telling herself that compared to everything else that had happened to her in the last few days, a handful of gadgets like these were hardly jaw-dropping sights, but she couldn't help being more than a little impressed. A Mapping Module? A Bumpass? A Pathwinder? Now these were inventions to put Josh's games consoles to shame! You're getting what you wanted, she told herself as Mr Pitts heaved his rucksack on to his back again, this is shaping up to be one kerrazy conundrum of an adventure. She set off after the funny little man, who'd begun striding purposefully past the rocks that marked the edge of the hilltop, and down into the encroaching darkness towards the tree-lined ridge beyond.

The Sun Flash Solarium

With the light almost completely gone, Millie and Mr Pitts were able to make good progress towards the Sun Flash facility without worrying about being spotted by any of Trooper's security team. She did have a few concerns about the nocturnal beasts they might encounter (she might be able to calm a lion down but that didn't mean every other predator on the savannah would be inviting them round for tea and biscuits) but thankfully they made it across to the tree line without meeting anything nastier than a porcupine, whose sharp spines persuaded them to give it a wide berth. They crept up to the crest of the ridge and peered over.

Millie had been expecting to be shocked, but she was so appalled by the sight that now greeted her she dropped her binoculars to the floor. Hands shaking, she picked them back up and took a deep breath, before scanning the landscape before her again. They were crouched on one side of a huge, bowl-shaped valley with trees and rocks encircling all but one small end of it. The valley floor below occupied a space about the same size as three or four football pitches laid out end to end, and was enclosed by a metal fence the height of her school hall with barbed wire curled around the top. Huge floodlights were perched on top of four enormous metal towers that stood at each corner, illuminating the ground below. In the middle of this arena stood a long, low building that stretched across almost the entire width of the space, with no windows and just one entrance that she could see – a set of sliding doors at the near end facing her, with two burly gun-carrying security guards stationed on either side of it. On the land to the right of the building lay six huge, flat black screens, each tilted slightly in the direction of the setting sun and emitting a low humming sound that could be heard from their hiding place in the trees. A thick cable ran from the corner of each panel to a gulley along the middle of the field and back to the building. *Those must be the solar panels*, thought Millie. She'd seen plenty of similar looking structures on family holidays to Cornwall but always on a much smaller scale; these were monsters in comparison.

The field to the left of the central building was the one that made Millie's stomach lurch, though. A handful of accommodation sheds were clustered in one corner, but the vast majority of the space was taken up with row upon row of enormous diggers, wrecking balls, shovellers, and earth moving machines, each of which had something unpleasant poking out of it – a line of sharp metal teeth, or a menacing spike. Millie lost count after she'd got to 50, and realised there must be hundreds of vehicles out there altogether – enough to do serious damage to the land around them. As she watched, she spotted the headlights of a pair of coaches approaching the complex from a distant road that ran through the only opening in the valley. They drew up alongside a gate set into the fence – manned by two more immense guards – and out stepped about fifty black-clad people, each carrying a duffel bag. The guards opened the gate, gesturing towards the accommodation blocks, and the people filed in.

"Welcome to the 'Solarium', as Trooper likes to call it, Matthew", whispered Mr Pitts. "You were right; it looks as though they're staffing up swiftly for the final phase. That'll be security – the heartless men and women happy to take Trooper's blood money and obliterate the planet's most beautiful creatures by herding them into their death-ditches. The next lot to arrive will be the additional solar engineers to make the panels, followed by the drivers. According to our mole, they're going to clear the land in a matter of a few brutal hours. As I said before, Trooper hasn't told the authorities the full scale of his plans and is banking on the fact that by the time they notice he's destroyed half the Serengeti the whole world will be addicted to his new game and it'll be too late to do anything about it. But given that I only found out the new deadline from you myself about an hour ago, I'm guessing the mole isn't aware of the change either. We'll have to tell her."

Mr Pitts dived back into his backpack, this time pulling out a half-eaten cheese sandwich and a few rungs of an old rope ladder (the rope at each end was broken and frayed), before finding what he was looking for. What emerged next was yet another peculiar-looking object. It could have been mistaken for a wooden recorder or flute, with holes along one side of it and a mouthpiece at the top, but instead of an opening at the bottom it ended in what looked very much like a large conker shell, complete with green flesh and spikes.

"Now, stand back, Mouldy – this can sound pretty unpleasant to the untrained ear."

Mr Pitts blew hard into the strange contraption, covering and uncovering the holes as though he was playing a particularly complicated melody despite the fact that no noise was coming out of it, then stopped and held the device high above his head by the mouthpiece. The silence continued for a moment, then the green flesh at the other end of the tube split open into three wedges (again, like a conker), and a tremendously loud trumpeting sound boomed out across the valley.

Millie covered her ears as the cacophony echoed from one side of the valley to the other.

"What on earth was that?" she said when her ears had stopped ringing.

"That, my friend, was a Herdle. So called because to the ignorant listener – by which I mean the sort of person who's not particularly interested in the natural world and therefore won't be paying proper attention – it sounds something like a herd of elephants.

"All bar one of the people down below us are ignorant listeners, so they won't have given it a second thought, but our mole will know exactly what's going on. Come on, we'd better go and meet her."

Gee Gee

Millie and Mr Pitts scurried along on the safe side of the ridge until they were in line with the sliding doors of the main building far below. The floodlights had been turned on as the dusk gathered, making their hiding place even darker to those within the Sun Flash complex itself, but with only one access door in evidence and two great apes guarding it, Millie was at a loss about how Mr Pitts' colleague from the Society of Extraordinary Adventurers was going to escape for a secret meeting.

No sooner had this thought finished crossing her mind when the earth she was standing on bounced once, briefly, like a toddler-sized trampoline, there was a brief but distinct twanging noise, and her hair was swept forward by a waft of warm air that came from the hillside behind her. She turned around, slowly.

Staggering to her feet beneath Millie and Mr Pitts was a very tall lady with very long, straight blond hair, and a pair of green-rimmed glasses, wearing a lab coat and carrying a clipboard. As they watched, she straightened out the hem of her coat, and ran her hands through her hair, which looked as though it had been blasted by a supersonic hairdryer, before taking a few tentative steps towards them, as though the ground beneath her might still be a bit wobbly.

"She must have used a flipwire to get to us" whispered Mr Pitts "it's a way of travelling very short distances using a similar transference pathway to the subsoil journey we made, but using the energy of the earth to flip you over the top of it rather than through it.

"Miss Gibbons, how are you? Used the old 'flipwire right next to the main entrance as it's the last place anyone would think to look for it' trick, I see!"

"Armitage, dear! How splendid it is to see you, and what a relief it was to get a Herdle from you so I could escape for a few minutes. I can't tell you how hard it is, living amongst all those vandals." The lady gestured towards the Sun Flash complex. "Yes, I've managed to hide a flipwire in a storage cupboard down there; it's a bit rough and ready but it serves its purpose well enough."

She turned her attention to Millie.

"And who do we have here? A niece? A work experience student? A horribly lost girl guide?"

"Miss Gibbons, meet our newest recruit, Millie Barton. Millie, meet Miss Gibbons – an expert electrical engineer and the Society's finest mole", said Mr Pitts, but before Millie had a chance to even register her surprise at being called the correct name for once, Miss Gibbons continued.

"Ah, a cadet – how wonderful! Call me Gillian, or better still, Gee-Gee. Now, what can I do for you both? I told my supervisor I needed a bathroom break, but she'll get suspicious if my piddle takes longer than 5 minutes."

"I'm afraid I bring bad news, Miss Gibbons" said Mr Pitts. "I don't know whether you know this, but Trooper's decided to launch his game in 5 days' time instead of 10, so we have even less time to stop him than we'd hoped."

"Oh, crumbs." exclaimed Gee-Gee. "I thought something might be in the air when they started increasing our shift hours last week. Despite my best efforts to sabotage their progress they've worked out how to rotate the solar panels over the course of each day far more quickly than they'd anticipated, and with such a greedy monster as Trooper in charge it shouldn't be any surprise that he's keen to get going as soon as possible. What on earth are we going to do? Now, let me think…"

She paused. Mr Pitts glanced at her expectantly.

"Right. I was hoping to test this but there won't be any time now, so I'm afraid we'll have to go in blind. It'll have to happen on the day of the great clearance, so everyone's contained. How many troops have we got?"

"Just two I'm afraid, and you're looking at both of them" Mr Pitts replied, looking at his feet. "You came here via the Sun Flash recruitment process of course, so you've only seen the overground route, but the subsoil pathway only allows two travellers at any one time. I was going to sneak a unit of members in two by two over the coming days but there's no time to rearrange that, now.

"However, Millie here is a Catastrophe. So I think there might be a chance we could build our army that way…"

Miss Gibbons stared hard at Millie for a few moments, as though she was working something very important out in her head. Finally, she spoke.

"We need a groundswell."

"Of course! You're fantastic, Miss Gibbons!" Mr Pitts exclaimed, perhaps a little more enthusiastically than he'd intended given the embarrassed flush that immediately appeared on his cheeks.

"A groundswell. Yes, I think that's the way we can do it," Gee Gee continued. "You see, Millie, this valley formed here because it's located on an area of weakness in the earth's crust. It's not a volcano as such, but there's a huge amount of earthy energy stored right underneath that main building, and if we can pierce the ground in just the right place it'll cause a chain reaction – a groundswell – that ends up with rocks and huge clods of earth forcing their way through the surface. The process will ultimately turn the valley into a huge hill, and it'll undo every last bit of Trooper's work. I think there's a hatch in basement room 372 that should give us the access we need to unlock the procedure. Set some charges in there, leave the hatch open and boom – down the whole thing comes.

"At the same time, we'll need to block off the entrance to the valley somehow, so no Sun Flash workers can escape, and they're trapped until the authorities arrive.

"Given our various skills – my knowledge of the facility, Millie's animal husbandry, and your geological skills, Armitage – we'll split the work as follows: I'll lead the way to room 372, Armitage can plant the explosives to set off the groundswell, and you, Millie, you'll stop the escapees."

Gee-Gee took a moment to let the plan sink in, then smoothed her lab coat down once more, clutched her clipboard to her chest, and started backing towards the shrub that she'd landed on.

"Right, that's piddle time over so I'd better get going. Although come to think of it I do actually need a piddle now so it's going to be an uncomfortable few hours for me until I can ask again. See you in five days, chaps. And best of luck!"

With this, she jumped backwards onto the bush, and with the smallest hint of a flipping motion she vanished. Millie stood there, dumbstruck.

"Okay," said Mr Pitts. "That sounds clear enough. Let's head back home before your absence is noticed."

So, I need to lead a team of animals to capture hundreds of Sun Flash employees single-handedly while the only two adults I know out here are trying to create some sort of earthquake-volcano, thought Millie. The plan might be clear, but the chances of it working must be slimmer than the chances of winning Trooper's stupid game in the first place.

A Spot Of Bother

D aylight had disappeared completely by now, to be replaced by a night sky so full of stars Millie wondered how there was enough space for them all to fit in. The sight was breath-taking, and Millie would've loved nothing more than to lie on the ground, staring up and taking in the wonder of it all until the sun reappeared the next day. However, she couldn't really allow herself that luxury as she was on a potentially world-saving mission. Also, Mr Pitts was rapidly marching away ahead of her, gripping one of the Bumpasses he'd introduced her to earlier firmly in his hands, and was in danger of vanishing from sight completely. She reached into her bag to retrieve her own contraption, and sure enough, as she ran her hands around its edge, she felt one of the rubbery studs that dotted the rim pulsating beneath her fingers. The stud in question was pointing towards the rapidly disappearing Mr Pitts now, and as she gently turned the disc in her hands, she felt the pulse move from one stud to the next, so it was always in line with the direction in which he was walking.

Millie was so focused on the disc in her hands she failed to notice that Mr Pitts had stopped until she very literally bumped into him. For such a small man, he was remarkably sturdy, she thought to herself as she staggered backwards; he hadn't moved a muscle when they collided and was stood stock-still. As she regained her own senses, she swiftly realised exactly why he'd immobilised himself. Rather unfortunately, it looked as though they'd headed into another potential Cat Attack.

No more than a few metres in front of Mr Pitts sat something at once both beautiful and terrifying, familiar and strange, cuddly and *what on earth are you talking about there's no way I'd go near that thing with a barge pole*. The creature in question was a leopard. And it was staring very hard at Mr Pitts.

Millie gulped. She felt her hands shaking. She was more scared at the sight of this lone animal than she'd been when they'd encountered the trio of lions on her first trip. Perhaps it was the leopard's eyes flashing in the starlight. Perhaps it was the way the animal was resting on its haunches with one paw held aloft, as if its next move could either be an ear-clean or a swipe. Or perhaps, Millie thought, it was the fact that it was seated beside the battered and bloody body of an enormous ostrich that had obviously been providing it with a supper of champions before these meddling humans appeared. This situation would require the serious employment of her newly discovered catastrophic skills, which she fervently hoped wouldn't let her down, this time.

She rested one hand on Mr Pitts' shoulder, slowly peered over, and cleared her mind, which is rather like clearing your throat, only instead of phlegm, you cough out all of the thoughts floating around in it.

Good evening, Mr Master Mrs or Ms Leopard, she began, a little hesitantly. *And may I just say what a fine evening it is!* (*What on earth are you doing?* she thought, hopefully only to herself. *Speak like a normal child, not like some toffee-nosed colonial snoot who's turned up here on safari!*)

Sorry, I'll start again. Look, I'm really sorry to have interrupted your delicious meal, or just to be clear, a meal that you're finding delicious but that neither I nor my companion here would ever dream of eating on account of it not really being to our taste. We're more burger and chips people to be honest (*Stop waffling, Millie!*). *But we're on a mission to put an end to what's going on in that valley behind us, and need to get back home to sort out a few things before coming back to finish the job.*

At the mention of the valley, the big cat's ears pulled back, and it growled, softly, causing Mr Pitts to flinch ever so slightly. Millie took a breath in her head and continued.

So, if we promise not to disturb your big bird there (…despite it having some extraordinary feathers that would be amazing in my collection – concentrate, you idiot!…)*, would you mind very much if we just, well, continued on past? Please?*

The leopard continued to stare for a few, tense moments. It placed both front paws on the ground, pushed its hindquarters up in the air as if to stretch them, then, to Millie and Mr Pitts' great relief, sat itself down to the ground on all fours and watched, as they half-walked, half-tiptoed, around the ostrich.

They'd got a few paces out of sight when they heard the unmistakable sound of four furry feet trotting towards them. For a moment, Millie thought she'd got her little speech horribly wrong and they were about to be attacked. The leopard reappeared at their side, then skipped ahead and stopped directly in their path. It took two paces towards them, then lowered its head and dropped something to the floor. It was an ostrich feather! Millie was so excited that she forgot herself and reached out to pick up the feather while the leopard's powerful jaws still hovered centimetres from the ground. But instead of biting off a couple of digits, the big cat simply nuzzled her hand, and, amazingly, *purred*.

Thank you, Millie whispered in her head. *We'll be back soon, don't you worry.*

Twenty minutes later, Millie and Mr Pitts had reached the rocky hilltop. Mr Pitts, who hadn't stopped chattering about the extraordinary experience they'd just shared since they left the company of their new found feline friend, folded the Mapping Module up and stuffed it back into his backpack along with his Bumpass. The Module must have been what was making his load so heavy, as when he hauled it on to his back he started staggering around in circles while he attempted to balance its weight evenly across his shoulders. He pirouetted on one leg, then the other, grabbing at any branch or rock within reach to try to steady himself, before eventually, Millie had to dash over and steady him. Despite the darkness around them, she couldn't help spotting a slight flush of embarrassment spread across his cheeks.

"Ah, thank you, Millipede," he coughed, "I think I must have strained my back in the subsoil, usually this thing's as light as a feather for me."

Mr Pitts directed Millie back to the landing zone rock ("always best to return via the line you arrived on to be honest – travellers have been known to pick up bits of each other's personalities by accident when they've swapped in the past"), and with a firm jump in exactly the same spot her bottom had landed on a few hours ago, she was catapulted back into the subsoil and up and out through the slats of the hamster wheel in Criceta's Emporium with a triumphant fart. Mr Pitts followed shortly after (with an even more impressive boom from his bottom), swinging back down from the top of the inside of the wheel with alarming speed due to the weight of his backpack. They dusted themselves down, and headed back in to the front of the shop.

"Right then, Millord," said Mr Pitts firmly, already mapping out the next steps of the plan in his head. "You'd better get back to your house before your parents return and ground you for even longer, but I'll need you back here on Saturday morning in plenty of time to make the lunchtime transfer. In the meantime, I'd better get to work making the explosives that'll unlock the groundswell. Don't be surprised if you hear a few nocturnal bangs and crashes in the Harpleford area over the next few days, but don't be alarmed, either. Well, unless you hear an explosion so loud it launches you out of bed as you sleep, of course. Then be very alarmed and please rush over to the shop to help me.

"Good work tonight, by the way; you're ticking all the Society's boxes so far. Although of course if you fail the next stage the whole planet's going to be destroyed in any case, so however many boxes you've ticked will be irrelevant. But still, well done! And I'll see you on Saturday."

With this, Millie was not unkindly but firmly shoved out of the front door of the shop and back on to Harpleford High Street. She dashed back home, arriving unnoticed by Josh and closing her bedroom door just in time to hear her Dad's car pulling up on the drive.

Farewell, Family

Millie woke before dawn on Saturday. Given that this was almost certainly going to be the most exciting day of her entire life she could perhaps be forgiven for this. She was filled with the nervous excitement that she'd only really felt first thing on Christmas Day before, when she'd usually wake up wondering whether her regular breaking of the 'don't stray too far from home' rule had left her sitting on the naughty or nice side of the man in red's list. Still, there were a good few hours for her to spend making a few important preparations of her own before heading to Criceta's.

First, she needed to find exactly the right outfit to wear. In the end, she opted for what she felt was classic adventurer chic: brown denim dungaree-shorts that offered toughness, camouflage, and plenty of storage in a big pocket-pouch at the front. She also spent a considerable amount of time in front of the mirror, practising a variety of appropriate adventurer faces: observant, determined, angry and victorious all came fairly easily to her, but unfortunately scary didn't – the best she could manage was one eyebrow raised, nostrils slightly flared, and one corner of her lip curled upwards, which made her look more like she was concentrating very hard on doing a poo. Finally, she unpacked and repacked the backpack she'd been given on her last trip four times. It contained an awful lot of stuff that most people would classify as 'rubbish' but given the various crazy contraptions Mr Pitts had shown her so far, she thought it best not to throw anything away, although she did add a pair of her own binoculars to the mix. While she was stuffing the last few bits into the bag's pockets for one last time, she heard her parent's door opening, followed by the familiar sounds of her dad grabbing his work clothes from the guest suite and charging downstairs. He was always exactly the same level of rushed if he was on an early Saturday shift, and Millie could almost guarantee that if she was hearing this routine it must be about half past seven now. She glanced at her watch and smiled – it read 07:32.

She joined him downstairs as he was wedging a

slice of slightly undercooked toast into his mouth and preparing a travel mug of capsule coffee to take with him. He looked her up and down. "Fluth par froo fairy, Frills?" he asked her.

Millie was pleased to notice that her translation skills were switched on this morning, "What am I wearing, Dad? Well, I've spent a good bit of time online this week – like you suggested – and this look is based on a jungle adventurer theme I've seen a lot of my favourite Youtubers rocking. I thought it might be a sensible thing to wear as I'm thinking of going to the, er, playground this morning."

"Very good" – he said, more distinctly now that he'd demolished his toast. "It suits you, lovely, it really does." Millie's dad gave her a twinkly smile as he spoke; the type of smile that didn't come around very often but carried an extra wallop of love and a sprinkling of mischief in it when it did.

"Make sure you take care, won't you" he added. "Those *playgrounds* can be remarkably hazardous." There it was again, the flash of a sparkle in his eyes. With a shout of "Bye, loves!" up the stairs, he grabbed his car keys, and shot out of the front door.

Millie made herself a hearty breakfast of porridge with blueberries sprinkled on top, a banana, and a couple of chocolate-chip cookies (the biscuits were needed purely for extra energy, she told herself), and was just polishing it off when her mum bounded downstairs clad from head to toe in neon pink and black exercise clothes, the worst aspect of which being the word 'booty', which was printed boldly across the back of her leggings. The general overwhelmingness of this vision meant that Millie's own outfit was positively invisible in comparison, so Millie didn't have to think of any more excuses for wearing it.

"Happy weekend, darling!" she exclaimed in an over-excited voice. "Isn't it a beautiful day! Perfect for a boot camp!"

Millie's mum had recently joined a local exercise group who seemed to enjoy spending two hours every Saturday morning over at the school playing fields being shouted at very loudly by a scary man with a shaved head, tattoos from his legs right up to his *face*, and arms the size of tree trunks. Millie didn't quite understand what made someone who wouldn't tolerate anyone raising their voice to her on any other day of the week pay money to have someone do it to them during their precious time off, but as long as it was going to keep her distracted, she didn't care.

Mrs Barton spent a few minutes preparing a particularly disgusting-coloured smoothie of frozen fruit, spinach, a raw egg and something called acai seeds which she told anyone who'd listen were 'the superfoodie's superfood' but which looked to Millie like a bag full of iron filings. She screwed the lid tightly on to the bottle, grabbed her cycle helmet from the cupboard in the hall, and was also on her way.

That left just Millie and Josh in the house. Millie hadn't heard a peep from his room all night, and she was pretty sure he wouldn't emerge even if he did wake up, given that these were the last few hours of rest he'd have before his marathon gaming session began at 11.59pm on the dot, when every Flash Pack on the planet was due to be delivered to its new owner simultaneously. Millie couldn't really bear to think about what he was going to do if the S.E.A plan worked and the Sun Flash console failed to arrive or start up later. If he ever found out she was even partly responsible, he'd never forgive her. Despite the fact that they were polar opposites in so many ways, Millie couldn't help being terribly sad at that prospect – they did occasionally share a joke together (usually at their parents' expense), they walked to school together (admittedly in silence) each day even though they didn't have to, and they'd even been known to hold hands if they were watching a particularly emotional film on TV. *Still*, she thought as she left the house and softly closed the door behind her, *Josh will survive no matter what happens. If I don't go through with this, there are entire species that might not be so lucky.*

The Mission

E ven by his own standards, Mr Pitts was in a particularly strange mood when Millie got to the emporium. When she'd arrived, he'd been wedged between the top outside edge of the Rotatormate 3000 and the ceiling, waving his arms around and waggling his legs in a forlorn attempt to unstick himself. Apparently, he'd been making final repairs to some of the less secure slats on the wheel and in order to reach the higher planks had jumped a little too enthusiastically, propelling the wheel into motion and taking him up to the ceiling with it. Millie had to grab one of his flailing limbs and yank on it as hard as she could before the wheel finally admitted defeat and rolled him back down to the ground.

Next, he grabbed the sacks of rodent bedding from the storeroom wall and tore them open one by one, scattering sawdust and straw all over the floor. As if this wasn't bizarre enough behaviour, he proceeded to open the filing cabinet drawers and pull out the reams of paperwork from inside each one, ripping the contents into shreds with his hands and adding this to the piles beneath them. By doing this, he told her, he was hoping that if their return journey went a bit wrong and they re-entered the room at high speed, they might at least save themselves from breaking any bones or bruising their bottoms by landing on this makeshift cushion.

Finally (and this was the weirdest thing of all), he fetched every last hamster from its cage in the front of the shop and carefully placed them one by one into a long plastic tube that rested on one of the shelves that ran the full length of the storeroom. It looked like a particularly fat, round gutter, with wire mesh sealing the entire length of the top so nothing could escape, and a small gate at one end which he shut once the final animal had been safely tucked in. Millie remembered him mentioning the unique tendency of hamsters to bottom burp in the presence of subsoil transference pathways just in time to clamp her hand over her nose. The gutter tube, which had been rocking from side to side madly as the animals were placed into it, became eerily still as the last rodent was inserted and the gate clicked shut. There was a pause for a second, before a buzzing noise like an extremely high-pitched kazoo filled Millie's ears and, through the minuscule gaps between her fingers, a smell invaded that was so nose-rottingly awful and so throat-strippingly disgusting it made her retch and would undoubtedly have had her vomiting, were it not for the quick thinking of her companion. Mr Pitts spotted her distress and waved a grubby handkerchief at her, which she gratefully tied around the lower half of her face like a highway robber as she saw he had also done. The handkerchief itself stank to smithereens of grease, hamster hair and (Millie was pretty sure) mouldy, mildewey jam of some sort, but this was such an improvement on the gassy pong she wasn't about to complain.

"What did you bring them in here for?" she asked, her voice a little muffled through the material.

"It may be that we have to, er, take off from this location rather suddenly on the way back, Margaret. So I need to have them close by just in case we need to hot-foot it out of Harpleford. Don't worry though, I'm almost sure we'll be fine – it's just a precaution."

Millie nodded uncertainly; as she was learning, it probably wasn't wise to believe Mr Pitts' reassuring words too much.

By the time Mr Pitts had finished getting the

storeroom ready and had unpacked and repacked their rucksacks – treating his own very gingerly as it now contained a large amount of explosive material – the clock on the wall read 1.54. So with only a few minutes to go before the two o'clock international transfer window opened, they completed their final preparations. For Millie, this meant checking the straps on her bag, the laces on her shoes, and the plaits in her hair to make sure she wasn't about to fly half way around the world at great speed with a loose cord flapping around behind her just asking to be snagged on a protruding piece of rock or an animal's snout. For Mr Pitts, it meant performing a series of stretches and lunges that would've given Millie a fit of the giggles had they not been about to embark on such a serious mission.

First, he used his right hand to pull his right foot up to his right buttock, as Millie had seen her Mum do after a boot camp session. Then, he leapt up in the air and attempted to pull his left foot up to his left buttock using his left hand at the same time. Needless to say, this was impossible, so he ended up slamming into the floor on his knees with a whimper each time he tried it. Next, he attempted a series of star jumps, but his feet kept sinking into the shin-deep sea of shredded paper and animal padding he'd thrown on the floor, so he looked more like he was frolicking in a pile of autumn leaves than actually leaping anywhere. Finally, he stood completely still with his forefingers firmly wedged in his ears and blew the loudest raspberry he could manage (which was impressively noisy). This, he declared, would clear his nasal passageways and ensure he could easily discharge any dirt that he picked up during a particularly hazardous transference journey. Millie felt dizzy just watching him, but before she had a chance to recover, it was time to get the great wheel turning again.

The journey through the Underwhere was familiar by now, but it still thrilled Millie to see the sparks whizzing by. She travelled second this time, and was relieved to make a smooth landing on the drop down. She was also relieved not to see any lions or leopards, not to be thwacked in the face by a springing tree branch, and not to find Mr Pitts knocked out on the rock, crushed by his rucksack, or exploded into smithereens by its contents. Instead, he was sitting quite comfortably in his landing zone, with his enormous bag balanced neatly behind him, breathing a little heavily but otherwise looking okay.

"Very nicely done, Milford!" exclaimed Mr Pitts. "Right, now there are plenty of clouds overhead, which will help us remain hidden, but it'll be fully dark when we return, and we may come back separately (Millie gulped at this), so I'd better give you a few pointers about how to use the Bumpass. Ha! Pointers!

Like a compass points! Ha!"

Once he'd got over the hilarity he'd caused himself with this unintended pun, Mr Pitts went into a lengthy and very detailed list of instructions Millie would need to follow in order to use the Bumpass correctly. She understood very few of these beyond the fact that she needed to squeeze a small button on the middle of the bottom of the device once for north, twice for east, three times for south four times for west, and five times to return to the mapping module. Leaving Millie to practise, he headed off to the tree to set the module up securely in place as before, then burrowed around in his bag for a long time, fiddling with the explosive devices he'd brought with him a little too roughly for Millie's liking. After what felt like at least an hour he'd finished setting up, and beckoned for Millie to join him as he headed off towards the Sun Flash site. They walked quickly in silence, each focused on their own role in the task that lay before them.

They reached the outside of the valley in good time, but instead of heading up to the ridgeline together as they'd done on their previous visit, Mr Pitts held his hand up to stop Millie going any further.

"Your mission is that way, young lady" he whispered, pointing towards the eastern side of the valley.

"Remember, you'll need to use the Bumpass to

help you navigate, the Pathwinders you've got in your bag to guide our animal helpers in the right direction, then your Catastrophism to enlist their help in securing the entrance to the facility.

"In the meantime, I'll be heading into the main building with Miss Gibbons to try to start the groundswell. As soon as you hear the first rumble from the valley floor, that's your cue to start closing the gates, or initiating lockdown, or whatever you'd prefer to call it."

With no more than a quick flash of a thumbs up and a half-encouraging, half-desperate smile, Mr Pitts was gone, disappearing through the trees that lined this side of the slope up to the ridge. Millie was alone, with only her barely tested language skills and a dozen balls of bait on sticks to help her. Everything around her was silent, broken only by an occasional distant howl, grunt, or the rumble of a low-pitched roar. *Right then, you lot*, Millie announced silently to whatever creatures were out there, *time to get this show on the road.*

A Rather Large Problem

illie's Bumpass knowledge was tested immediately, as she headed up into the trees in a direction she hoped was east, towards the narrow valley entrance. She didn't reach the very top of the ridge but picked out a route just below it to make sure she couldn't be seen from the other side. Despite the darkening sky above and the foliage surrounding her, the way ahead was illuminated thanks to the glow from the huge spotlights. She could hear noises now: the deep-throated cough and rumble of engines being kicked into life, the beeping of vehicles reversing, and an occasional shout from an irate site foreman.

The ridgeline started to curve around to the right up ahead of Millie, and she could make out the metal frame of one of the huge floodlight stacks up ahead. If her memory was correct, the valley ridge started to drop down to the floor immediately after that frame. Sure enough, as she got close enough to the structure to be able to make out its criss-crossing poles in more detail, she also noticed the shadows of the trees becoming thinner as the ground started to fall away to the valley floor. She turned slightly to her left, and clambered down to the bottom of the slope as quietly as she could manage.

Millie could see the line of the single road that ran into and out from the valley by the light that spilled out from the complex within it; it looked unearthly, like a laser beam being projected from an alien craft in one of the games Josh enjoyed playing so much. It was about a couple of hundred metres away at most. *Right, then! Time to start unpacking those Pathwinders*, she thought.

She took off her rucksack and opened it up, reaching in to collect the three sticks contained inside. Bearing in mind she hadn't yet removed the wrapping from the top of any of them yet and seen the effect this produced, she was understandably a little nervous when she'd laid her hands on the first one. She felt for the stick and ran her fingers around the brown paper wrapped around the ball at the top, being careful not to rip it. *Here goes nothing*, she thought as she bent down to pull it out.

She heard the crunch of a twig behind her, turned, and suddenly everything went dark.

Grunt

"Well, ain't this just peachy. Ain't this a whole new *level* of downright dirtiness and darn duplicitousness from that bunch of looney tunes and crackpots at that there Society of Madventurers! I know *all* about them and their ridiculous planet-saving ideas from my threat-research department. They really must be running low on members if they're having to send scrawny scraps of kids like you off on their ridiculous schemes, is all I can say. What's your name, RUNT? And what the hell do you think you're doing poking around in my back yard?"

Millie blinked hard, as the scratchy and horribly whiffy hood that had been covering her head since she was grabbed out of nowhere by the entrance to the valley was ripped off her head. She'd been firmly shoved onto a chair, with her hands tied behind her back, in a small, windowless room. This was the sort of room that only nasty things happened in, and as is the case in all such places, the chair was screwed to the floor, as was the table that sat in front of her.

The question had been directed at her from a distance of no more than 10 centimetres in front of her, by a sight that would've been revolting at 10 metres, no, make that one hundred metres away. Jeremiah Trooper – pink-faced entrepreneur, overweight environment wrecker, and, it turned out, genuine contender for the world's most stinky-breathed human ever, leaned over the table in front of Millie, his forehead striped with rivers of sweat, and spit flecking the corners of his mouth. He truly was hideous outside and in, she thought, as he at last took a step back to await her response.

"I'm Millie. And I'm here to stop you," she tried to say in her most confident voice, although it came out in a bit of a rush and she squeaked a bit at the end, so it sounded more like "ImillieanIherestipyou."

"Whas' that? Here to Stop me? Ha! Let me correct you there. First of all, I prefer the name Runt, as that's exactly what you are. And second of all, you're not here to stop me, you're here to *try* to stop me. And you have *failed*. See, when you were sniffing around the entrance to my little Solarium here, you somehow didn't notice the small – or should I say large – matter of my very finest henchwoman creeping – or should I say stomping – up behind you. Runt, meet Grunt."

Trooper gestured to the wall to his left, against which stood a hulking brute of a woman. Dressed from head to toe in black, with wraparound sunglasses wedged on top of a head of jet black hair pulled back tightly into a fearsome high ponytail, and wearing a belt from which dangled a variety of objects including a truncheon, a walkie-talkie and (Millie gulped) a gun holster, she was twice as wide as the door she stood guard at, and so tall she had to lean back against the wall to stop her head hitting the ceiling.

"Grunt's real name is Gwendolin – she's one of your Welsh countryfolk – but she don't talk too much, and when she does I can't hardly understand the dang fool, so Grunt seems more appropriate. She spotted you on the security cameras earlier and headed straight out to have a looksie. I'd have thought she'd have had a bit more trouble catching you on account of you being an 'adventurer' and all, and her footsteps being heavy enough to set off earthquake monitors, but I guess you're not quite so smart after all, are you?"

"It doesn't matter who I am," Millie interjected, managing to keep her composure even though inside she was burning with humiliation, "what matters is that you're not going to get away with your despicable plan."

"My despicable plan, huh?" scoffed Trooper. "Now let me guess... you think my despicable plan involves getting every kid on the planet addicted to Trooper's Treasure Tunnel so I can make even more money, huh?" He didn't wait for a response before continuing. "Well, that just goes to show that you're even more stooopid than I thought. And I thought you were pretty darn stooopid in the first place!

"My plan, Runt, is far more sophisticated than that. See, I'm as rich as Elvis already. I'm as rich as your queen. Hell, I'm as rich as both of them combined! I don't need more cash-o-la; even if I gave away the trillion-dollar prize on day one I'd still have more money than I'd know what to do with in a thousand years. No, see, I'm far less superficial than a lot of folks believe. I'm a thinker. A real, deep, thinker. And I've been thinking about how to come up with a game like this for an awful long time.

"I mean," he continued, really getting into his stride now, "it's true that kids are gonna end up paying more than they thought the game was gonna cost them. It comes free on the Flash Pack, sure, but you have to pay for extras just like in so many other games, and what right-minded parent wouldn't pay a few bucks to give their kid an advantage when the prize is so big?

"The brilliant thing is, though, that as the prize is *so* crazy big, folks will get their dumb heads mixed up and stop keeping track of the money their little brats are spending. Even if they do look at how much they're paying out, parents are gonna fool themselves (or their kids will fool 'em) into thinkin' they've gotta be contenders for the trillion, so really, what does it matter if they keep spending, and spending, and spending every last penny they have on the thing. It's an investment, right?"

He paused and wiped away a tear of laughter. *He really does think everyone on the planet apart from him is stupid, doesn't he*, thought Millie.

"But," he added, "it's not an investment, is it? It's a sure-fire road to ruin! I guarantee that as a result of my genius game, all over the world houses will be repossessed, savings will be obliterated, jobs will be lost, families will go hungry. And this" – he paused to make sure he had Millie's full attention – "this, is when things *really* start to get interesting.

"See, when people truly have nothing, when their families have nothing, when their neighbours have nothing, when their friends have nothing, then you might just find that all this silly, soppy 'I care so much for my friends... Oh I love my wuvely family so much I just want to burst' nonsense that everyone spouts on their social media accounts these days, all goes out the door, and you're left with a world in which people start looking after the only person that truly matters. Numero uno. Your solo, selfish self.

"Nobody will be clicking 'follow' or 'like' online any more. There won't be 'neighbourhoods' in the real world any more. There won't even be 'families' any more. It'll be a case of every man, woman, and child for themselves, and everyone will finally understand what I've always understood. Which is what it feels like to be truly, deeply alone."

Silence fell. Trooper was lost in his own thoughts – in the memory of his childhood, perhaps. It was clear to Millie that this was where his awful ambition had been born; having had parents who barely noticed he was there when he was a boy must have scarred him terribly. Still, she thought, there were millions of people on the planet who'd had far worse upbringings than him, and they hadn't decided to take out their frustration on the world in such a terrifyingly bonkers way. No, she couldn't muster any sympathy for the man – his 'poor me' act wouldn't work on her. She had to try to think of a way out of this room, and fast.

"Aaaanyhoo," he continued, tapping his watch, "we're on a bit of a time-critical schedule here, so I'm going to have to get back to the whole 'Operation let's kill all the animals, make me even richer, and destroy civilisation as we know it while we're at it', thing…"

He started towards the door.

"Wait!" Millie shouted at his back. He paused, and turned back to her.

"I know I've failed. I know there's no point in me trying to stop you. You win. You've already won. You're going to get your own way, and the world's going to change forever. But…"

She paused, desperately trying to think of something else to say that might delay or distract him a little longer. Her own part in the mission may have gone wrong, but she might at least be able to give the others a bit more time to do their bit.

"Say what now, Runt?" said Trooper, impatiently.

"But… But unless you want to blow up your entire operation here, you'd better dispose of my, er, 'Ground Grenades'. They're in my rucksack."

S.O.S.

Trooper stopped in his tracks. He nodded to Grunt. "Grab that bag and bring it over here." Then, turning to Millie with a nasty glint in his tiny eyes, he added, "Let's see if our little adventurer here's talking nonsense, or if she's really gone and got herself some explosives in her schoolbag, shall we? Turn it out."

The huge beast of a woman undid the top flap, and shook the contents of the bag on to the table. Out fell Millie's Bumpass, along with the other supplies she'd packed back at home, which felt an awfully long way away now. Amongst the jumble of weird and wonderful objects sat the three Pathwinders. Millie had to admit, they did look quite grenade-like. Under the close scrutiny of Grunt, she picked all three up and held them out towards Trooper.

"DON'T WAVE THE DANG THINGS AT ME, RUNT!" he screamed, waddling hastily backwards to keep as far away as possible. "WHADDYA EXPECT ME TO DO WITH THEM! GRUNT! DO SOMETHING!"

A plan was finally forming in Millie's mind. "Please calm down, Mr Trooper" she said. "The idea *was* to detonate them inside the valley here, and they're set to go off in" – she looked at her watch – "23 minutes from now." Trooper's pink face went as white as a sheet. *Brilliant*, she thought, *he's bought it. Now let's try to get things back on track.*

"But the thing is, that they need to be near a power source like the Solarium here in order to work. If you put them outside the valley entrance, they'll fizzle out with no more of an explosion than a bunch of party poppers. Get them out of here in time, and you'll be safe."

"You'd better not be messing with me, Runt" Trooper growled. "If this is some sort of time-wasting trickery, you'll be sorry. Grunt, pack everything up again and dump the bag outside the valley entrance. I'll wait in the control room and watch you on the monitors from there." He drew his face close to Millie again, leering over her. "And YOU can go with her. Grunt may be an almighty waste of space in a lotta ways, but her size is pretty useful from time to time. So you can be my insurance policy, making sure I don't lose her as a result of you 'accidentally' giving us the wrong instructions."

With that, Grunt swept everything back into the rucksack, dragged Millie up and out of her chair, and marched her towards the exit. "Be quick," Trooper said as they headed through the door (Grunt had to turn herself sideways to squeeze through), "we need her back for the final act. I'd hate her to miss it."

Millie was marched through a maze of corridors before heading out of the entrance doors they'd observed during their previous visit. The fresh, savannah air was tainted by the reek of diesel from the huge machines that surrounded them, and she couldn't stop shaking in the looming presence of her minder. The plan she'd worked out was far from guaranteed to work, and she had no idea how Mr Pitts and Gee Gee were getting on.

Grunt was very definitely not a talker. In fact, she hadn't uttered a word since she'd become acquainted with Millie by throwing a hood over her head earlier in the evening. This suited Millie perfectly, as it meant she could plan her next move more carefully. It also meant that she was free to observe everything that was going on around her, and what a terrifying sight this was. The whole of this side of the complex was buzzing with activity as the hundreds of construction, or rather *destruction*, vehicles lurched into life and were checked over, before being assigned a driver. They were filling up fast; it'd be no time at all before the whole fleet was ready to be sent out into the grasslands beyond.

Millie and Grunt reached the valley entrance, and Grunt pulled hard on the cord binding Millie's wrists to stop her.

"Ouch! There's really no need to be quite so forceful, Ms Gwendolin" complained Millie, hoping that confident, strict politeness might help her get away with her next move. "We can drop the grenades here, but we'll need to plant them firmly in the ground, so they don't get picked up and carried back into the complex by accident. Give one to me, and I'll show you how it's done." Millie's bet paid off – Grunt obeyed the instruction without question, untying her ropes, opening the rucksack and gingerly handing over one of the Pathwinders.

"You simply place the pointy end in the ground like this, then remove the protective covering like this" – she ripped off the brown paper before Grunt had a chance to do anything about it – "so that, er, the explosives don't overheat, and, er, explode. Understood? Good. Let's get on with the others, then."

Grunt eyed the now exposed ball that was sticking a few centimetres out of the ground with what might have been described as suspicion. She blinked twice, very slowly, then picked the next Pathwinder out of the rucksack and slowly copied the procedure. It seemed to take all her powers of concentration to follow these simple instructions, thought Millie, which gave her another idea as she grabbed the third and final stick from her bag and plugged it into the ground. All three devices were now placed outside the Sun Flash complex, and all three were live. All she needed was a bit of time to try to communicate with the creatures whose attention she'd hopefully just attracted.

"Thank you, Ms Gwendolin," she said to her dim-witted companion, "now all we have to do is to wait for precisely one and a half minutes to make sure the devices have been successfully neutralised. The only thing is, I can't remember how many seconds one and a half minutes would be. Can you figure it out?"

A panicked look crossed Grunt's face, and a strangulated "grrullp" emerged from her mouth, as the enormity of the task she'd just been asked to help with started to sink in. Her eyes rolled back up into her head as she began to grapple with the mathematical challenge she'd been set. Millie had bought herself some time, but who knew how long it might take for Grunt to come up with the answer?

Just as she'd done on her first trip to the rocky hilltop, Millie opened her eyes wide, took a deep breath through her nose, and prepared to address whatever creatures were hopefully making their way through the darkness towards the Pathwinders at this very moment. She strained her brain as hard as she could, until sparks danced in front of her eyes and she could hear the blood coursing through the veins in her forehead. If she'd have been making any sound, she'd have been shouting at the top of her lungs. But she was silent, communicating through her thoughts alone.

This is a Save Our Savannah call – an SOS – to every cat that calls these lands their home. WE NEED YOU NOW! I don't have time to give you the whole story and I know none of you even know who I am, let alone whether you can trust me or not, but I'm deadly serious when I say that if we don't stop what's in the valley behind me from getting out of the valley behind me you're all going to either lose your homes, your food, or your lives! So please, please, follow your noses to the valley as fast as you can. We might only have…

"Grunt? GRUNT? Get back here now you stoopid lump! And bring the girl with you!" Trooper's voice crackled through Grunt's walkie-talkie, snapping the huge hooligan back to attention. Millie's time was up; all she could do now was hope her message had reached the wildlife beyond.

Rounded Up

""Welcome back, Runt" laughed Trooper, standing in front of a bank of television screens in a room buried somewhere deep within the complex. "And welcome back, Grunt! Ha! Grunt and Runt! I got me a rhyme!" *Creative thinking obviously doesn't come easily to the man*, thought Millie, *but why on earth is he quite so pleased with himself? Surely it's not just because he's decided he's a poet?* She didn't have to wait for her answer.

"Allow me to introduce you to one of my most diligent employees. She used to work in our electrical development team but recently it seems she's decided to offer her services to the maintenance guys, as she's been scurrying around poking her nose into all sorts of areas that are *way* beyond her security clearance. One of my guards first spotted her in the central generator hub a couple of three weeks ago and ever since then we've been following her everywhere. Well, I say everywhere, but we haven't exactly followed her to the bathroom – we're not animals, after all! Anyway, I've got a feeling you might already know her. Come on in, Miss Gibbons."

The door to the monitoring room opened and in came the pitiful sight of Gee Gee, accompanied by another of Trooper's henchmen, with her hands tied in front of her and her eyes to the floor.

"We just found her messin' around with one of the hatches in the basement level. Elvis only knows what she was doing there but whatever it was obviously couldn't be carried out alone, as she needed a partner – and looky who we have here!"

What came next was even more upsetting, as Mr Pitts was led limping into the room, looking even more dishevelled than usual. He too was bound by ropes at the hands, and was clearly in pain.

"This fella here was inside the hatch! My team had to yank that leg good and hard to pull him out of there. Sorry 'bout that, er, Mr Putz, was it?"

"Pitts" came the adventurer's reply.

"Ah yes, Pitts. Well, you're certainly in *them* now ain't ya – ha!" laughed Trooper, warming to the idea

143

that he was some sort of comedian.

"Now, I could ask you what the HECKY DECKY you were doing down there but you know what? I'm busy, I'm bored of y'all already, and it really doesn't matter in the end, as number 1) I'm about to become even more extremely rich and powerful, and number 2) you're about to become even less extremely irritating and alive.

"I've got myself a great little research team here, Pitts, and they've given me a quick heads-up about your own background. You," he waved at him dismissively, "are something of a loner. No family, no friend who'd miss you if you vanished… heck, you're a lot like me! In another life we'd have been kindred spirits! And as for you, Miss Gibbons, your contract of employment here states in no uncertain terms that Sun Flash can't be held responsible for any accidents that occur if you stray beyond your permitted workspace. You've certainly done that, so if you were to happen to get fatally injured then there'd be nothing anyone could do about it. So, here's what's going to happen. Given that you're such good buddies, you're both going to pay a visit to some of our poorly patients in the animal welfare centre. Have a look at this screen here and you'll see exactly what's in store for you, folks!"

The monitor Trooper showed them next chilled Millie to the bone. It showed a bare room as big as a school hall, with nothing in it but three very big, and plainly very angry lions. They were quite unlike the beasts they'd seen on the rock. Keen-eyed, lean, and mean, they looked unhappy, and scariest of all, hungry.

"The runt's another matter. If she didn't get back in one piece her parents would get all upset and call the po-leese, and who knows where that might lead. So you, my lucky girl, will be shipped out of here in my private jet – in the luggage hold, of course – and delivered right back home. It's up to you what you tell your parents when you get there. You can tell 'em the truth if you like, although you'll probably get grounded for a month; let's face it, no one's ever going to believe the *real* story here, particularly as my clean up squad's going to demolish this Criceta Emporium of yours as soon as the game's been launched, Pitts."

So this is it, thought Millie as Mr Pitts and Gee Gee were led back into the corridor in front of her. *My friends are in life-threatening danger, and this time there's not a thing I can do to help.*

The Animal Welfare Room

"Time to say goodbye! Adios! Sayonara! Toodle-pip, or whatever it is you Brits prefer these days. But you'd better make it quick, I've got a show to watch! Who knows, maybe 'Savannah Destroyer' might make a neat title for my next game?"

Trooper had led them at pace, waddling and wheezing back through the maze of corridors and down to an underground level which housed the ominously titled Animal Welfare Room. It was about as inconspicuous a door as you could imagine, with a small sign attached to the front of it, and a hatch set into the wall on one side. The door was unguarded and didn't have any keypad or locking mechanism in place. Of course it didn't, thought Millie; nobody in their right mind would open it given the creatures lurking on the other side. Trooper noticed her looking at it and laughed. "We only ever need to open it if we've got unwanted guests who need to pay my friends inside a visit, and the animals are so 'enthusiastic' to greet them they don't really give 'em a chance to get to the handle on the other side once they're in there. Rest of the time we just slip 'em a few bits of buffalo steak through the feeding hatch here. We, uh, may have forgotten to feed 'em for the last few days, what with all the final preparations for launch and all, so I should imagine they'll be pleased to have some fresh prey to hunt. Come on now, you two, don't be shy!"

With that, Grunt slowly turned the door handle and the two thugs who'd been guarding Mr Pitts and Gee Gee started pushing their prisoners through the door as it was very carefully opened. The captives resisted as much as they could, which wasn't a great deal in their current state, but their actions did allow Millie a few precious seconds to focus her attention on the big cat presence she could sense further into the room and scream at the top of the voice in her head:

Stop! Please don't hurt my friends! Help them and they'll

help you get out of here! They'll free you! Help th…

This was all she managed to get out before the door was clamped shut, and silence descended.

"Don't worry, Runt, it's soundproofed on the other side, so we won't hear any icky stuff from now on. Anyhoo – like I said, I've got a show to watch, so I'll just say see you never again, and head off to watch my finest work take shape. Grunt, come with me. And you two" – he gestured to the other guards – "get Runt off to the airstrip and send her back home to face the consequences of her make-believe adventure."

With that he was off and away, up a flight of stairs further down the corridor, with his huge minder in tow. Millie, meanwhile, was distraught. She slumped to the floor outside the Animal Welfare Room, quiet sobs racking her body as she contemplated what her friends were going through, and her own wretched failure to save them. The guards let her sit there for a few minutes, then took hold of her arms and lifted her back up to her feet, before starting to head back in the direction they'd come from. Aside from the sound of their feet shuffling along, all was silent.

Apart from the noise of a door handle being turned, that is.

Three Lions

Millie was so lost in her own despair she barely registered the noise to begin with. Her guards did, though, and with their faces turning white they glanced first at each other, then back down the corridor to the welfare room door. Sure enough, the handle was turning, then the door was opening, and out stepped Mr Pitts and Gee Gee, immediately pressing themselves against the corridor walls as three magnificent lions tumbled out behind them, stopping, sniffing the air, and turning their heads to survey their surroundings. They looked at Millie, silently acknowledging that she was on their side, then at the guards, who clearly weren't. Even if these heavies had been as slow in the brain department as Grunt, it would've been obvious to them that they were in trouble – snarling big cats with fangs bared, lowering themselves onto their haunches ready to pounce will give anyone a sense of impending danger. They turned and fled around a corner, pursued by two of the beasts. The third and biggest cat remained behind, sitting up and staring at Millie as though waiting for further instructions.

Thank you, my friend, thought Millie. *Could you be terribly helpful and go to find Trooper? He's the big, pink, ball-shaped man who's been keeping you shut in here – I'm sure you've seen him before –and he just went up there,* she pointed back towards the stairs along the corridor. *Find him, and trap him if you can. Oh, and obviously thank you most graciously indeed for not killing my friends!*

The lion flicked its head, turned, and trotted off. Mr Pitts, meanwhile, had rediscovered his voice and was jumping up and down on the spot, pressing both hands to his temples.

"The explosives! We can still get them going if we're quick! Get us to room 372 again Miss Gibbons, on the treble! Oh, and, er, thank you, Millennium. I owe you one, yet again."

Gee Gee was plainly still in shock from her near-death experience and the sight of a small child communicating with three lions, but she nodded and strode off smartly back up the corridor, closely followed by her two companions. After a few twists, turns, gangways and stairways, they found themselves in room 372, with the hatch that Mr Pitts had talked about firmly closed in front of them. The three of them grabbed its enormous handle and heaved it open, revealing a small tunnel heading down and away into the depths of the earth beneath.

"This is actually a garbage chute, Millie," explained Gee Gee, having regained her voice as the terror she'd been feeling had turned to a thrilled excitement that their mission was back in business. "But what the idiots who built this place didn't know is that it also sits directly on a faultline in the ground beneath, which in turn will act as a key if we give it a bit of encouragement, unlocking the groundswell we need to get rid of this whole place once and for all.

"Can you still see your device, Mr Pitts?"

While Gee Gee was talking, Mr Pitts had launched himself almost entirely into the hole, with only his feet still poking out of the top.

"Bwll frmm Mrp Grbbb! Hraaaaa!"

With this bizarre series of noises complete, Mr Pitts catapulted himself back into the room.

"Sorry about that. I said, 'All fine Miss Gibbons. Hurrah!'"

"So you've located the explosives and set the timer?"

"That I have, Miss Gibbons. Slight problem,

though. I couldn't reset the timer so was only able to restart it again. And 27 of its 30 minutes have passed already. So we only have three left to get out if we don't want to be buried under here forever."

Neither Gee Gee nor Millie needed to hear this more than once. All three of them bolted from the room, led by their lead MOLE, and ran until their lungs were burning, back through the corridors, up the stairs to the ground floor, and finally out through the entrance doors of the facility, where they faced a sight unlike anything any of them had ever seen before.

Mayhem

*S*o this is what the word 'mayhem' was invented to describe, thought Millie. *And perhaps the word 'chaos', and probably a little bit of 'carnage' as well.* As the entrance doors slid open, a wall of noise burst through, assaulting Millie, Mr Pitts, and Gee Gee's eardrums with a cacophony of shouting, siren-wailing, crashing, and banging. As they turned right, towards the valley entrance, the source of the commotion became crystal clear. At first, it seemed as though every single one of the hundreds of construction machines out here was in motion in some way or other. Some vehicles were racing across the few patches of unoccupied ground around the sides of the valley, waving their bucket-fronted arms around in an attempt to clear a new pathway, while others were frantically revving their engines to try to get over one of the numerous obstacles that now lay strewn across the landscape, caused by fallen or abandoned building supplies. Most of the machinery was grouped tightly together, though – formed into a huge triangular wedge with its point facing towards the valley entrance. Millie could almost feel the weight of the huge crush of metal and rubber, as each vehicle ground itself into the back of the one in front, trying to force its way through. But why was the air so heavy with desperation? What was making Trooper's workers so keen to escape the complex? Casting her eyes along the valley walls, Millie got her answer.

Lining the top of the ridge that sloped upwards on either side of the distant road was an entire army of cats. Hundreds of lions, cheetahs, leopards, and even a few wildcats were spaced evenly down the hillside, still, and silent, but possessing the sort of malevolent power that could bring a sudden end to the lives of every living thing in the valley below. Millie's part of the plan had worked! The animals must have picked up on her broadcast, or felt the pull of the clump of Pathwinders, or both. How they'd known to spread themselves out and take guard in this way was beyond Millie's understanding, but for now, all that mattered was the fact they'd come to help.

There was a maze of pipes and guttering attached

to the side of the main building, and using all the skills she'd developed as an expert tree-climber, Millie scrambled up them to the roof to get a better look, pulling out her binoculars when she got there. At the entrance to the valley, where the scrum of vehicles narrowed to single file as they tried to get onto the road beyond the gates, stood a queue of perhaps seven or eight stationary diggers, all of which formed an impenetrable plug that the machines behind simply couldn't dislodge. They'd been deserted, their drivers chased out by the same family of lions that Millie and Mr Pitts had run into on their drop-down zone, whom she could see now, pinning maybe a dozen of the workers to the gated fence. She scurried back down the pipes, eager to tell Mr Pitts about the coincidence. She didn't quite get the enthusiastic response she was hoping for.

"That's all very well, Military" he said, a bit abruptly for her liking. "But it doesn't exactly help our own escape plan, does it? And where, for that matter, is Trooper?"

At that moment, their conversation was interrupted by a rumble. Not an 'I've just woken up and crikey I need a blueberry pancake' stomach-rumble. Not a 'very old school bus full of children trying to get up a very steep hill' rumble. But a primal rumble, deeper than the bass boom of an oil tanker's horn, emanating from deep within the bowels of the earth, and making the ground beneath them begin to vibrate like the worktops in the Barton's kitchen when their washing machine was having a particularly energetic spin.

"It's starting!" shrieked Gee Gee, excitedly. "Well DONE, Armitage!" She grabbed Mr Pitts on either side of his face and planted a kiss squarely on his rather high forehead. Despite the chaos surrounding them, he blushed. "Er, ah, hmmm, thank you Miss Gibbons" he stuttered, "but really it was a joint, eerrr….!" He was saved any further embarrassment by a huge, violent *whumpph*ing sound from the middle of the valley floor. This was followed by a tremendous creaking and groaning noise, before the far corner of the main building was suddenly thrust violently upwards, folding the metal roof panels back on themselves and ripping the side walls in two as though they were made of paper. The back section of these walls wobbled momentarily, before collapsing down onto the floor under the weight of a cascade of rocks that seemed to be pushing themselves out of the ground like an enormous pile of profiteroles. They watched, mesmerised, as the rocks kept appearing, spilling out and crushing everything around them, and started to fill up the valley just as Gee Gee had predicted.

"The flipwire!" yelled Mr Pitts. "We can use it to launch ourselves to safety! Although of course," he continued, apparently to himself but evidently forgetting that he was still shouting, "it's not been tested for three, so we might end up slamming face-first into the fence, plus the groundswell has quite conceivably twisted the pathway, so we could land in the middle of the chaos over there, or on a broken tree stump, or even into the mouth of a lion. And of course it might have simply snapped altogether, so we might just be buried alive in the building as the rocks rain down on us, but let's not tell the others that."

Gee Gee and Millie shared a look, as if to agree to pretend they hadn't heard the last bit. "Good idea, Armitage," said Gee Gee, "Follow me, chaps!"

The three adventurers scrambled back around to the front entrance of the building to a small storage cupboard just inside the entrance that was thankfully still standing for the time being. Gee Gee pulled hard on the door, which squeaked an objection but opened wide enough for everyone to enter. A strip light flickered above them, providing only a dim illumination of their surroundings: a length of hosepipe attached to a tap on the wall, a stack of buckets, a bundle of mops, and a shelf full of loo rolls. On the floor in one corner stood an extremely out of place musty old leather armchair. It was one of those old reclining ones, with a lever on the side that had to be pulled to activate a footrest below.

"Here we are, Millie," said Gee Gee, walking over

to the armchair and tapping it proudly, "hopefully this'll be our ticket to safety. I found it hidden behind a desk in the reception area. Had a bit of a job on my hands getting it into this place, but it was worth it – she's got a good bit of propulsion in her. I call her bouncing Belinda."

Mr Pitts raised an eyebrow at the sight. "Ah, no disrespect, Miss Gibbons, but it's not exactly a Rotatormate now, is it? Do you really think it'll take all three of us?"

"We don't actually have a choice, do we, Armitage," snapped Gee Gee, clearly not in the mood for his constant worrying. "Now, grab that hose and let's get started."

Mr Pitts knew exactly what Gee Gee was intending to do, as he disconnected the hosepipe from the tap on the wall, shepherded Millie over towards the armchair, and started winding the tubing around all three of them where they stood, binding them together tightly until they could barely move. Next, with a one, two three, *heave*, Gee Gee and Mr Pitts shuffled and lurched sideways until they all flopped onto the seat, their legs and arms everywhere, and with Millie's head buried rather unfortunately in Mr Pitts' very ripe armpit.

"Okay," said Gee Gee, who had fortunately managed to get herself on to the top of the pile, "Millie, I think you're on the side of the lever. Find it, and grab it, now."

Millie fumbled around, and sure enough, she soon located the hard metal stump. "Got it", she shouted into Mr Pitts' armpit.

"Right, now wiggle it for all you're worth. We're relying on you, young lady!"

Millie's arm was half-bent behind her back so moving the lever even a tiny amount was rather tricky at first, but she somehow managed to get going, wobbling the stick back and forth, and extending and retracting the footrest as she did so. What on earth this had to do with them escaping death by rockfall was beyond her, but she'd been around the Society of Extraordinary Adventurers for long enough now to understand that what made sense in everyday life didn't apply here, and vice versa.

After a minute of frantic waggling, and despite being given plenty of encouraging noises from her companions, Millie was exhausted. She was about to give in, when Gee Gee suddenly shouted "Bounce, Mr Pitts, Bounce!" and Mr Pitts, who was squeezed beneath both of them, uttered an enormous *"GAAAAAAH"* and pushed all three of them up and off the chair, causing them to fall back down heavily onto the seat cushion just as the footrest was on one of its outward, opening movements. Millie felt as though a huge hook had been looped around the hosepipe that bound them, just before being yanked up out of the seat and into the air.

She barely had time to question why she hadn't hit her head on the ceiling of the store cupboard, or to register the sensation of flying on what felt like an invisible bungee rope before, with a tremendous crash, bump, and roll, she found herself tumbling down the outer side of the valley, just below the ridgeline. She heard an almighty "*Goooooooof*" as they came to a rest against a tree trunk.

"I may… *ooh*… have cracked… *aaargh*… a rib or two there, Miss Gibbons", moaned Mr Pitts, who'd been unlucky enough to be at the front of the bundle of adventurers when they hit the tree, "but at least we're out, eh?"

"Quite right, Armitage, and thank you for your chivalry," Gee Gee winked at Millie as she said this. She began to unravel the hosepipe from around them. "Thank goodness the old flipwire worked, eh?"

The three of them staggered to their feet and crept towards the ridgeline. The rumbling was louder now, and they could hear the sounds of the groundswell continuing its work, but they still needed to see if they could spot Trooper amongst the devastation.

The scene on the valley floor was even more dramatic now. The rocks had continued to burst out of the opening in the ground, covering all but the entrance funnel to the complex, and forcing the workers to flee their machines and into a huddle on the road beyond. The big cats had moved down from the valley sides to encircle their human captives, trapping them as securely as if they'd been locked in a jail cell. The adventurers scanned the crowd for Trooper, but despite his huge bulk, his unnaturally bright skin, or his enormous bodyguard, they struggled to find him. Then, suddenly, Millie shouted, "Look up!" and pointed towards the lighting tower that overlooked the entrance.

About three-quarters of the way up its frame stood a square viewing platform made of wooden planks, and around this patrolled the great lion Millie had sent off to find Trooper. Just above it, clinging on to the iron girders that rose towards the top of the tower, trembled the pea-eyed, pink-faced despot himself – trapped, with a birds' eye view of the destruction of the complex below.

Homeward

"You know it as well as I do, Armitage. One of us has to stay here to make sure the proper authorities turn up and sort everything out. I'll be absolutely fine; I'll settle myself on the ridgeline by the lighting tower, and when the fuss has died down, I'll hitch a ride back to the nearest city then slope off back home in a more, well, conventional manner. Don't you worry about me – I've been doing this almost as long as you have, after all."

Gee Gee was attempting to calm down a rather distressed Mr Pitts, whose romantic feelings towards her were becoming slightly more obvious now that the most stressful part of their experience seemed to have come to an end.

"Well, okay, but you must send word as soon as you're back home. Please. I'll be, er, worried."

"But of course I will, dear Armitage; how will you be able to invite me for dinner, otherwise? Goodbye, Millie – and welcome to the Society!"

With that tantalising invitation, Gee Gee skipped away into the trees, leaving Millie in the company of a seriously flustered Mr Pitts.

"Right, I, er, yes, so, hmmm," he began, before Millie took pity on him.

"Shall we get going, Mr Pitts?"

"Absolutely, Michaelmas. That's it – let's get going. Bumpasses at the ready!"

Off the pair of them went, jogging back towards the drop-down zone with renewed energy now they knew they'd avoided their own demise and had achieved their savannah-saving aims. They were so happy at the success of their mission, and so full of delight at their own brilliance, they briefly forgot their caution – laughing and woo-hooing their way through the open plains. They were so jubilant, in fact, that they both failed to notice the bulky, black-clad figure that stalked the darkness behind them.

An Uninvited Guest

"Grunt!" screamed Millie. They'd reached the clearing at the top of the hill and were setting themselves up for the return journey when she'd appeared on the slopes below, looming up behind the rocks, stretching out her huge limbs to climb up as quickly as she could, her usually expressionless face twisted into an angry sneer. She didn't have to speak to make it abundantly clear that she was not happy about what had happened to her boss, and was seeking revenge on his behalf.

"Oh, rotten hamster farts!" exclaimed Mr Pitts, using a curse that was clearly one of the most extreme that any member of the Society of Extraordinary

Adventurers might utter. "There's nothing for it, Malteaser, we're going to have to go home in tandem. I'll be right behind your behind. So please accept my most sincere apologies in advance for any accidental headbutting of your bottom that might occur on the journey. And just make sure you get clear of the Rotatormate as soon as you land!"

He hastily retrieved the mapping module without bothering to turn it off, while Millie got herself into position, then managed to get himself to his own landing place on the rocks just as Grunt's torso appeared at the other side of the clearing.

"You go on the count of three, I'll go on the count of five. Or perhaps the count of four and a half," he added, nodding towards the rapidly advancing figure beyond. "One, two, three…"

With that, Millie jumped up, and back into the subsoil, careering back with no thought to the wonder of her surroundings this time, just filled with a desperation to get home, and alert to any sign of Mr Pitts' bonce on her backside. Luckily, he didn't manage to catch her up, and she rocketed into the store-room of Criceta's Emporium on her own, rolling back down and out of the Rotatormate 3000. When he still hadn't shown up thirty seconds later, she started to worry. And when a full minute passed, she escalated this worry to full-on panic. She was about to step back on to the giant wheel, disregarding any rules about agreed travel times in order to head back in and try to retrieve him, when, with an almighty smash that shook the wheel from its fastenings on the floor and dislodged at least a quarter of its wooden slats, he appeared, groaning, and grabbing at his ankle as he rocked back down to the floor.

"She… nearly… caught me, Mabel," he gasped. "Grabbed my ankle just as I was jumping up to drop down. Even with her limited brain power she'll have figured something inter-natural is going on, so we have to assume our security here is compromised. Quick, help me fill her in!"

With this, Mr Pitts began ripping the remaining slats from the wheel, stuffing them into the hole in the ground, and adding the ripped-up papers and animal bedding he'd scattered on the floor earlier as he went. When the metal skeleton of the frame itself was the only remaining evidence of the Rotatormate, he dismantled this, too, wedging its poles into the hole and piling the electrical gadgetry on top of them. Finally, with as many obstacles as they could find wedged into the entrance to the pathway, they heaved the filing cabinet away from the wall and tipped it over, watching it crash onto its side on top of the hole, covering it. Silence descended.

"I don't honestly know if this will work, Millie," said Mr Pitts, quietly now. "If she deliberately or even accidentally gets herself into the subsoil, it may be the case that Grunt's head is thick enough to burst through everything we've shoved down there and back into this building. So, I'm afraid I'm going to have to follow the Society's protocols and evacuate the location. Permanently."

"What do you mean, Mr Pitts?" replied Millie, although she had a worrying idea about what her companion was about to tell her. She clung to the possibility she was wrong, all the time knowing she was, as usual, almost certainly right.

"I mean it's time for our adventure to end, my friend," he said, his voice dropping to little more than a whisper. "Although Trooper's been contained for now, he'll almost certainly bribe his way out of captivity, and then he'll come looking for the Society, starting with me and Miss Gibbons. For the sake of the organisation, I have to make his job as difficult as possible. Come, let's get ourselves out of here."

Mr Pitts walked over to the store-room shelves, where the hamster-filled half-tube still rested, squeaking and parping noises occasionally escaping from it. He picked it up and rested it over his shoulder, before heading out through the curtain onto the shop floor, then back out to the street. Millie followed, her eyes fixed to the floor, with her thoughts anywhere other than on the words they were about to exchange.

Outside, Harpleford High Street was as ordinary as ever; its residents going about their weekend business in blissful ignorance of the drama that had recently occurred on the other side of the world. They barely gave Millie and Mr Pitts a second glance, despite the shop owner carrying a long, farting drainpipe.

"So, er, this is, ahem, goodbye, Millie. On behalf of the Society, I'd like to thank you from the very heart of my bottom for saving me, saving the savannah, and almost certainly saving the world.

"You're quite wonderful, you know. Every child is, really, but you care about your planet in a particularly special way, and that makes you almost unique. You're the most deserving recipient of honorary membership of the Society of Extraordinary Adventurers that I've ever known; your name will be added to our roll of honour and if you ever want to join us on another mission you'll only have to ask – I'm sure you'll figure out a way to find us. I hope, more than anything, that our paths cross again someday."

With a nod of his head, Mr Pitts turned away from Millie and shuffled off, stepping into a nearby alleyway, and out of sight.

Millie stood there in silence for a full minute, then slowly turned around and headed back towards home.

A New Leaf

Back in the Barton household there was a noticeable excitement in the air, so much so that when she came through the front door nobody noticed the fact that it was well past Millie's bedtime or glanced at her bedraggled appearance. Josh didn't even have his head buried in his Gamebox, for once; instead, the whole family was crowded into the living room, the television tuned to a news channel with the words 'Breaking: Serengeti Sun Flash Slaughter Saved!' plastered across a banner running along the top of the screen.

"Millie, look at this!" said her Dad, pulling her into the room. "You know that Sun Flash console that was going to be the biggest thing ever to hit the world of gaming? Well it turns out that the company was involved in some sort of criminal misbehaviour in the Serengeti! The African authorities discovered it just in time to avoid an environmental catastrophe! And they managed to stop any of the devices themselves leaving the warehouses around the world – apparently, they were powered by some super-strength solar power technology, which the boffins at the UN are taking a look at to see if they can put it to good use instead.

There's a bit of suspicion some sort of secret agency was involved, though," he added, raising one eyebrow just a fraction, "and it looked as though there'd been a significant amount of big cat activity in the area, which is very peculiar. I'm sure we'll find out what that's all about eventually." He stared long and hard at Millie as he spoke, the slightest of smiles registering in the corners of his mouth.

"Oh, wow, Dad," she mumbled, "that sounds, well, extraordinary. And sorry, I guess, Josh. You must be gutted."

"Not really, Mills," her brother replied, "I've given up gaming for a little while. See, I was waiting on the doorstep for the Flash Pack to arrive when I had a bit of a turn. I think I had so much energy stored up in me from sitting in my room for so long – and perhaps from the three litres of sports drinks I'd downed earlier – that my body sort of took control of itself and I leapt up and started pelting around the garden like a demented dog. I only stopped when I'd climbed the highest tree I could find and couldn't get any higher. It was amazing. Oh, and I found this while I was up there – I thought you might like it."

He reached into the pocket of his jeans and pulled out a feather of the purest white Millie had ever seen. Her collection was complete.

Millie smiled, "Thanks, Joshie. Look, I'm sorry everyone, but I'm a bit worn out after running around outside all day, so I'm going to go up to my room. I'll be back down to say goodnight."

"Okay, darling – see you in a bit," said her Dad. "Nice rucksack, by the way."

In the rush to seal up the subsoil pathway and leave before Grunt could catch up with them, Millie had forgotten to hand over the backpack Mr Pitts had given her. As soon as she got to her room, she took it off and dropped it onto the bed. She hadn't had time to fasten it back up before the downside-up journey and most of its contents had fallen out, apart from the small, round disc with buttons bobbling around its edge. The Bumpass. She picked it up, remembering the amazing events that had been taking place last time she'd had it in her hands.

As her thoughts drifted, she felt a slight throbbing coming from one side. It was pointing towards her bedroom window. Of course! Mr Pitts hadn't turned off the mapping module, so it was still broadcasting from his rucksack! Millie turned and walked towards the window, looking out across the landscape beyond.

You're out there somewhere aren't you my friend, she said to herself. And I'll find you again, one day.

Acknowledgements

I've had more totally biased feedback and unconditional support than I could have possibly wished for while I've been creating Millie and her world. First and foremost, this has come from home; I couldn't have written this story if I didn't live in a house full to the brim with silliness and fun. I'm grateful beyond measure to Tamara, whose encouragement and assurances that "no, this is *not* a waste of time that could be better spent doing something more useful" kept me going, (even if we never did add that family walk to the mix). Zee Zee and Minnie, you know you're the reason I embarked on this adventure in the first place, and the thought of your laughter is what drives my writing. This is one hundred per cent your book.

Mum and Dad, thank you for showing me the

importance of nurturing children with respect, love and attention, and for sharing a love of language that will always be with me. Thanks too to Nilima and Jacek, for your matchless generosity towards the whole Strange crew. And thanks Hannah, Alka, Peter, and your many(!) wonderful children – your wicked sense of humour (senses of humours?) has given me more ideas than you can imagine.

'Write what you know' may be a cliché, but it's certainly true that although I don't happen to be acquainted with any pet shop owners or bank managers, I'm lucky enough to be surrounded by friends and colleagues who entertain, inform, inspire and educate me every day. There are far too many of you to mention individually, but as far as tips of icebergs go, thanks to Uzma Bozai, Geoff Dunster, Sean Garrehy, Simon Gill, Rob Glossop, Andrew Harding, Antonia Hodgson, Alex Lockwood, Sara Talbot, and Dean Tyler; if you think you might see yourself or your influence in these pages you're probably correct, so apologies for the thievery.

Printed in Great Britain
by Amazon